DIAMONDS
IN THE ROUGH

ERIC WALTERS

Stoddart Kids

*We acknowledge the Canada Council for the Arts
and the Ontario Arts Council for their support
of our publishing program.*

Published in Canada in 1998 by Stoddart Kids,
a division of Stoddart Publishing Co. Limited
34 Lesmill Road
Toronto, Canada M3B 2T6
Tel. (416) 445-3333 Fax (416) 445-5967
E-mail Customer.Service@ccmailgw.genpub.com

Published in the United States in 1998 by Stoddart Kids
85 River Rock Drive, Suite 202
Buffalo, New York 14207
Toll free 1-800-805-1083
E-mail gdsinc@genpub.com

Canadian Cataloguing in Publication Data

Walters, Eric, 1957-
Diamonds in the rough

ISBN: 0-7736-7470-5

I. Title.

PS8595.A598D52 1998   jC813'.54   C97-931859-9
PZ7.W37Di 1997

Cover design: Tannice Goddard
Cover illustration: Albert Slark

Printed and bound in Canada

*To all those teachers
who spend their careers finding diamonds
and making life less rough.*

◆

ACKNOWLEDGEMENT

It's unfortunate that people see the name on the outside and the words in the book and think one is totally responsible for the other. A novel is a story that evolves, changes and grows, and that growth is often facilitated by the help of people whose names are never mentioned. I'd like to thank Elsha Leventis, Kathryn Cole and Kelly Jones for their editorial work and the students of Plum Tree Park Public School for helping to breathe life into Cole and Sky. Thank you all.

Chapter 1

The knocking on the door startled me out of my sleep, and I sat bolt upright in the easy chair. I didn't know what time it was, but the television buzzed out a high pitched test pattern that let me know it must be really late because the station was off the air for the night. Mom was supposed to be back by midnight, but she was late more often than she was on time. I pushed the button on the remote to turn off the set as the knocking came again. Why was she knocking instead of letting herself in anyway? I guess she must have misplaced her house keys — again. She was always misplacing something. As I stood up and stretched the knocking came a third time, much louder than before. If she woke up the girls I'd be mad. It was hard enough to get the three of them into bed without her waking them up.

"I'm coming," I called as I rushed to the door.

"You're late! You were supposed to be home by —" I stopped short. It wasn't my mom standing there, but two policemen, looking awfully solemn.

"Sorry to disturb you," the younger of the two officers said. "Is this the residence of Rebecca Chambers?"

"Why?" I asked. I wanted to know what they wanted with my mother before I answered any of their questions.

"Are you her daughter?" the policeman asked.

"Why?"

The two officers exchanged a serious look.

"Can we step in so we can talk?" the older of the two asked. He was tall with a big belly hanging over his belt.

"I'm not supposed to let strangers in," I answered.

"We're not strangers. We're police officers."

"I don't know either of you two, so you're strangers to me."

The heavy one shook his head. "We need to talk to somebody. Can we speak to your father?"

"I guess you can . . . if you can find him." He'd been gone for so many years that I wouldn't even recognize him if I bumped into him in the mall.

"Look, kid, we don't have time for any of this," the chubby one said as he brushed by me and walked down the hall. "I need to speak to whoever's in charge!"

"You were just talking to her," I barked as I followed him. He had no right to just barge into our house!

"Sorry," the younger officer said, "it's just that it's important we talk to an adult. But we have to establish we have the right house. Is Rebecca Chambers your mother?"

"I already asked you, why do you want to —" I stopped mid-sentence. He was holding my mother's bright blue wallet. "Where did you get that?"

"Is this your mother's?" the officer asked.

I nodded. So that's what this was all about. She'd lost her wallet and they were just returning it.

"Is there somebody we can call? A grandmother, an aunt or somebody?"

"Nobody. But, why do you need to call anybody? Just leave the wallet and I'll give it to her when she gets in."

"Um . . . well, it . . . um . . . isn't that simple. What's your name?"

"Sky. Sky Chambers."

"Sky. Are you the oldest in the family?"

"Yeah."

"And how many brothers and sisters do you have?"

"Three sisters. No brothers."

"And they're all here?" the officer asked.

"Sleeping."

He turned to his partner. "Go make the call. I'll handle things here." Chubby looked as though he'd just won a free membership in the donut-of-the-month club. He retreated down the hall, his gun, handcuffs and baton jangling as he went.

"What's going on?" I demanded, my heart racing. None of this was making any sense. Where was my mother?

"Please sit down, Sky," he said as he eased himself into the chair.

"I don't want to sit down." I backed away from him.

"This isn't easy to say," he began, staring down at the floor. Why wasn't he looking at me? Why was he so nervous?

"Sky, there's been an accident. Your mother's car was hit . . . the other driver was drunk and he ran a red light . . . hit her broadside."

My legs went weak, and a cold sweat gripped my entire body. "Is she . . . all right?" I gasped in a whisper.

He shook his head slowly. "She's dead, Sky."

For some unexplainable reason, I laughed. The words didn't mean anything. He was wrong. She was just late. She was always late. She'd be home in a while, an hour or two later than she'd promised, and have some story about how the old heap broke down, or how she'd met an old friend and got lost in conversation or she'd have an injured bird or a scrawny cat under her arm. She was always stopping to help everything and everybody. And she'd peek out at me from under one of her silly hats, hair flying all over the place, and smile her goofy smile and apologize for being late and making me all worried, and then she'd promise never to be late again, and . . . and I knew . . . she wasn't coming home again.

The next few hours, and days, went by in a blur. We were taken to a receiving home, a temporary place to stay. People, strangers, told us where to go and what to do — and I was in too much shock to protest. I felt like I was hardly alive. They told us everything would be all right, that we weren't to worry, we'd be taken care of. And then, three days after the funeral, they separated us. Meadow and Brooke were sent to one foster home, Summer another, and I a third. And as I lay in bed that first night in my new "home," alone and unable to sleep, I swore that we'd all be together again and that I was going to make it happen.

* * * *

My hands were still shaking, but just a little, probably not noticeable to the others in the waiting room. I took a slow, deep breath. I needed to calm down, stay in control.

The clock on the wall clicked: 1:18. What was taking them so long? The meeting was supposed to start at one and my sisters weren't even here yet. Where were they? Had something happened to them? Panic gripped my gut and I felt the shakes starting again. I couldn't think about losing them too.

"Good afternoon, Sky. It's good to see you."

I looked up. Joanne was standing by the door. She was short and slight and very jittery. She reminded me of a nervous little bird.

"Please come in," she said. I ignored her, walking right past her and into a large room. It was empty except for a couple of desks against the far wall, and few chairs and a large wicker basket filled with toys in one corner. A mirror extended the length of the whole back wall. I found myself standing in a large, empty office.

My fear burned off in a burst of anger. "Where are my sisters? Why aren't they here?" I demanded.

"They'll arrive shortly. There's nothing to worry about," Joanne answered as she closed the door.

"I'll decide if there's something to worry about!" I snapped.

"The driver phoned to say he was running a little late. They're in good hands."

"No they're not. They're in foster homes. If they were with me they'd be in good hands."

"Sky, we've talked about this. You're only fourteen. You're their older sister, and not their mother."

6

"That's right, I am their sister — and you're nothing but some stupid social worker."

"It's normal to feel anger, and healthy to let it out," she replied in that sickly sweet social worky voice.

"Hah! In that case maybe I should show you just how healthy I am!" I glared at her.

She looked down at the floor. I walked the length of the room, stopping in front of the mirror. I turned away as tears started to well up in my eyes. They were never far away these days, but I wasn't going to let any of these people see me cry, wasn't going to let them see me being weak. I bit down hard on the inside of my cheek to chase away the tears.

I hoped my mascara was still okay. I'd had to put it on in the washroom off the waiting room. The stupid foster parents wouldn't let me wear makeup, and I needed it — my eyelashes and eyebrows were so thin and faint they were practically invisible. Part of the curse of having light red hair. Imagine those people thinking fourteen wasn't old enough to wear makeup! And I didn't even look my age — everybody thought I was at least sixteen. I guess I could live with it, or get around it, if that was the only rule, but there were rules for everything — curfews, bed times and mealtimes, having to tell them every place I was going. Stupid rules made up by stupid people. Maybe they were "foster parents," but they weren't my parents. They were just some people getting paid to keep me in their house.

I drew my hand away from my hair. It was just a habit, but when I was nervous I twisted my hair, around and around. I'd done it since I was a little kid. I had a hard enough time making my hair do what I wanted without getting it all balled up. Maybe if I had it cut shorter it might behave better. Still that wouldn't change the color. Why was I the only one in the whole family who didn't have blonde hair?

The telephone buzzed and I jumped. Joanne ran to answer it.

"Your sisters are here," she said, returning the phone to the cradle.

The door burst open and Meadow and Summer raced across the room. Summer threw her arms around me so hard I nearly toppled over. I hugged her back. Meadow stood quietly by my side. That was her way of saying it was okay for me to hug her, and I drew her close with my other arm. Over the tops of their heads I saw the foster parent, Debbie, walk in carrying Brooke. Brooke saw me and burst out laughing. She struggled to be let down and her feet hit the ground running. I pulled her into the center of us so we surrounded her, like a circle of wagons warding off an attack.

"Is everybody all right?" I asked anxiously.

"Everything's fine," Summer answered. There was no surprise there. Summer always thought everything was fine. It was almost impossible to ever see her without a smile on her face.

"Meadow? Are you and Brooke okay?"

Meadow nodded. I had to smile. She was wearing the same things she always wore — blue jean shorts, a shirt showing a soccer player kicking a ball through a net, and a New Jersey Devils baseball cap with her hair sticking out the back in a ponytail. They were her favorite clothes. Mom used to call them her uniform, and you had to peel them off her to wash them.

I looked at Debbie and Joanne. "You both better know I'm going to check every time I see them. Nobody better hurt them in any way or —"

"Nobody is going to harm them," Joanne replied.

"Not with me around they won't and that's why I'll keep on watching." I scooped Brooke into my arms. "Can we be left alone now?"

Joanne hesitated. Last week I'd threatened to take my sisters and run away, and they'd been watching us more closely since then, like they thought I might do it. I wouldn't really run away with them. Where could a fourteen-year-old girl run with her ten-, seven- and three-year-old sisters trailing behind? It would be different if I had a place to go or some money to get there, but I didn't. All I could do was worry them, and I liked worrying them.

"That's fine," Joanne answered. She opened the door at the far side of the room but stopped before leaving. "Please stay in here. If you need anything, call."

"Won't you know even if we don't call?" I asked. She looked confused.

"Aren't you going to be spying on us?" I asked, motioning to the mirror.

"It is one-way glass, Sky, but nobody will be watching you," Joanne replied.

"Sure, right," I muttered. I didn't believe her any more than I believed anything anybody said.

They left the room and Brooke and Meadow pulled out a plastic castle and some farm animals from the basket and started playing.

"Grab a chair," I said to Summer. We dragged two chairs across the floor and placed them close to where the two little ones were playing. I made a point of putting my chair so I was facing away from the mirror.

"Do you really think they're watching us?" Summer whispered.

"Probably not, but it doesn't matter. Have you heard anything about what they have planned for us?"

"How would I know anything?" she asked.

"Maybe you overheard them talking or something."

"I only know what Joanne told us before."

"Joanne doesn't know anything!" I said loudly, turning toward the mirror to scowl in the direction I thought she could be sitting. I hoped she was watching and heard me insult her.

"Joanne is nice."

"You think everybody is nice, Summer."

"Well . . . not everybody, I guess, but almost everybody."

"Most people are jerks. The sooner you get that in your head the better off you'll be."

"Wanna play?" Brooke asked. She shoved a wooden train into my face.

"Not right now, Brooky, I need to talk to Summer. We'll play later."

"Not later, now!" she demanded in her squeaky voice.

"Better play with her or she'll throw a tantrum," Meadow interrupted. "She's been doing a lot of that the last week, screaming and yelling if she doesn't get her way."

"Besides, there won't be any 'later,' Sky. The visit is only for an hour," Summer added.

"I guess you're right." I took the train from Brooke and knelt next to her.

It felt good to be down on the floor, playing, listening to Brooke making choo-choo sounds and watching Meadow putting the little wooden people into the castle. Summer started humming to herself, too fast and out of tune, just the way she sings. It made me smile. Suddenly I was struck by all the things that had happened. Was it only two weeks ago? Somehow it still didn't seem real.

I tried to stop them, but the tears started to come. Before the first one had rolled part way down my cheek, Summer wrapped her arms around me. Brooke climbed onto my lap and Meadow raced to one of the desks and returned with a box of Kleenex. That was just like Meadow, looking for a solution to any problem.

"It'll be okay, Sky, just you wait," Summer said.

"How . . . how will it be okay?" I asked, brushing away the tears.

"I don't know yet, but I know we'll all be able to live together again — soon."

"You're just dreaming. I don't see any way out."

"You've got to have faith. Things work out for the best, that's what Mom always said."

"Were you born and raised in Disneyland, Summer? Why can't you understand things aren't working out?"

"I just know we always got by. Things always worked out, just like Mom said . . . for the best," she replied softly.

"Does this seem like the best?" I demanded. "Mom's dead and we all live in different foster homes. Does that seem like the best?"

Instantly I regretted my words and the way I'd said them. Summer looked crushed and Brooky looked about to cry. Meadow had her back to me, her hands on the toys, pretending to ignore everything, but I knew she was listening too. I had to say something.

"I'm sorry. You're right, Summer, everything will work out, I promise." Summer smiled and the upset in Brooke's face faded. "I'll take care of it like I always do. Right, Meadow?"

"Yeah, yeah, whatever," she replied without turning around.

The door opened and Joanne and Debbie came back into the room. Our time together must be nearly up.

"A few more minutes, girls, and you'll have to leave," Joanne said apologetically.

I turned away. I stuck my finger in my mouth to wet it and rubbed under both eyes to remove any mascara that had washed down with my tears. I wished the mirror wasn't at the other end of the room so I could see if there were any tracks left.

"When do we meet again?" I asked.

"On Wednesday night," Joanne answered. "That's just two days. You'll all be having dinner and spending the evening together."

"We will? Where?"

"At our house," Debbie replied, flashing me a nervous smile. "If you want to come."

"Yeah, I guess that would be all right."

I stared at her hard. I'd been introduced to her but I couldn't remember her full name. Meadow and Brooke called her Debbie. I didn't call her anything. She wasn't very old, maybe in her middle twenties, and was sort of pretty and seemed nice enough to the kids.

"I thought it would be reassuring for you and Summer to know what sort of people are caring for your two sisters," Debbie continued.

"I know what sort of people are looking after them."

"You do?"

"Yeah. Foster parents. People who make money taking kids into their house."

"But we don't do it for the money," she protested. "Honestly, the money isn't important and it isn't very much."

"Then why do you take it if it isn't 'important or very much'?"

"Leave her alone, Sky!" Meadow barked. She put down the toys and glared at me. Meadow was only seven, but she was the most stubborn seven-year-old in the world. Why was Meadow defending this woman anyway? She'd only known her for two weeks and she was my sister. I swallowed. I wasn't going to get into a fight in front of these people.

"Yeah, sure. What time?"

"I'll pick you and Summer up around five," Joanne answered.

"And how do we get back home?"

"I'll drive you after the girls go to bed," Joanne replied.

"Where will you be while we're eating and visiting?" I asked, even though I figured I knew.

"Debbie has kindly invited me to join you all for dinner."

"Great, just great. Now I'll get indigestion for sure."

"Were you watching us?" Summer asked.

"Watching you? When?" Joanne replied.

"When we were visiting. Through the mirror."

Joanne shook her head. "Nobody was watching you. We'd never do that without telling you first."

Summer gave me a knowing look.

"Why do you have something like that?" Meadow asked.

"At times we have to observe visits."

"But why?" Summer asked.

"Well, sometimes we have to bring children into care to protect them."

"What does that mean?" Meadow asked.

"From getting knocked around," I answered. "You know, moms or dads hitting their kids."

"Yes, it's called child abuse. I know it must be hard to imagine, but some parents hurt their children."

"Yeah, real hard to imagine," I said sarcastically. I looked at Summer. She wasn't smiling anymore. Meadow's face was blank. I wondered how much she remembered about her father. Mom made him leave before Meadow turned two.

Her father, Earl, was good to Meadow but acted differently toward Summer and me. He started hitting us, mostly me, to teach us "how to behave." At first it was when we did things wrong, and maybe Mom didn't agree but she didn't stop it. Then he'd tear into us for no real reason, always when Mom was away. We didn't tell her anything about it. When she finally found out, the time he gave me a black eye, she went totally ballistic. For someone who believed in peace and nonviolence, she got pretty violent. She threw things at him and then started hitting him. She grabbed the phone off the table, ripping it out of the wall, and chased him around the room with it, swinging for his head. He dodged and ducked, but she finally connected with his jaw, and it knocked him for a loop. He picked himself up, raced across the room, out the door and down the front path, leaving a trail of blood.

The next morning I woke to find Earl's stuff on the porch. After breakfast I looked out again and his things were all gone. That was the last we saw of Earl.

Mom never hit us. She didn't believe in it, although with some of the things I'd got into I wouldn't have blamed her if she'd wanted to. If I'd been my daughter I would have given me a wallop. Of course, that would never be a problem for me since I was never going to have any kids. I'd had enough caring for my little sisters to ever want to raise any other kids.

"Before you go, I thought it might interest you to know the insurance claim is moving ahead," Joanne said.

The driver of the car that hit our mother was

drunk. He didn't get a scratch on him. The only damage he'd suffer was through his insurance company, which was being sued for her death.

"The lawyer thinks the settlement will be substantial," Joanne continued.

"Enough to buy us a new mother?" I snarled.

"I didn't mean that!" she stammered. "I just meant there'd be money to take care of you!"

"Will we be given the money?" Sumer asked. I could see Joanne was relieved Summer had asked the question. She liked Summer — but then, who didn't?

"No, it'll be put in some sort of trust fund, for when you're older, I think. We can't make any decisions about the money until we've exhausted all efforts to find your next of kin."

"Good luck." I prayed none of our fathers was going to be found. Summer and I had the same one, but Brooky and Meadow each had different dads. Mine had been gone almost ten years, and even Brooke's had disappeared over two years ago. We honestly didn't know where any of them were and the little information I did have I kept to myself. The things I did tell Joanne were made up to send her searching in the wrong direction. Finding any of them could mean we'd be separated, permanently, and there was no way that was going to happen.

"It's been hard with the limited information we've had to work with, but we've got to keep trying. That's the law," Joanne continued, looking me square in the eyes.

"Look all you want. You won't find anybody," I shrugged, staring her down.

"You never know . . . you just never know."

I didn't like the smug look on her face when she said that. Was something up?

"Oh, and Sky, I'd like you to stay around for a while after the others leave."

"Why?" I asked, my heart rising up into my throat.

"I need to talk to you about some of the difficulties you're having at the foster setting."

I felt a wave of relief. They hadn't found anybody.

"Sure, whatever," I mumbled and turned away from her.

Chapter 2

I looked impatiently at my watch. It was past five, and each passing moment standing here by myself on the street made me feel more exposed and vulnerable. The cars all seemed to be going so fast, and all I had to protect me was a few inches of concrete curb. How many of these drivers had been drinking? A car slowed down. It wasn't Joanne but some middle-aged guy giving me a look over. I flashed him the finger and he took off.

Before that jerk had disappeared from view, a sleek black BMW changed to the curb lane and slowed down. I watched out of the corner of my eye as it came to a stop. The windows were tinted so dark I couldn't see who was inside. I took a few steps back to get a little farther from the curb. Then the passenger window rolled down. If I had to I could run up the steps and into the foster home.

I bent down so I could peer in through the open window without getting too close. It was Joanne! I walked over and leaned in the window. The cool air inside wafted out at me.

"Get in. We're late!"

"Yeah, I know." I opened the door and settled into the seat. Before I could even pull on my belt, the car rocketed away from the curb and the window slid closed.

"Some car," I said, fumbling with the buckle.

"Yes, it is." Joanne kept her eyes on the road.

I looked around. Leather seats, CD player, instrumentation panel like a jet airplane. Expensive. Very expensive.

"Whose car is this?"

"It's mine."

"I thought social workers didn't get paid very much."

"We get paid all right."

"Enough to afford a car like this?"

"Well . . . maybe not that well."

"Then how could you afford it? You got a rich husband or boyfriend?"

"I'm not really supposed to talk about myself." Joanne sounded defensive.

"Why not? Are you ashamed of something?" I asked.

"No, of course not . . . it's something they teach us in our social work training."

"That doesn't make sense. You're always wanting me to tell you things."

"That's my job," she replied.

"Yeah, but don't you think I might be more willing to talk if you talked?"

"Well . . . "

"Tell you what, you answer my questions and I'll answer a few of yours."

She didn't say a word.

"So, do you have a rich husband?"

She smiled. "I'm not married. And I don't have a boyfriend."

"Big surprise," I muttered under my breath.

"What?" she asked, looking at me.

"Nothing. So how did you afford it?"

"It was a present from my father."

"Your father gave you a car! Why would he do that?" I asked in disbelief.

"It was a graduation present when I got my degree."

"Then it must be a new car."

"Yes, it is. It's only three months old." Joanne got a distressed look on her face. "Maybe I shouldn't have told you I'm just a recent graduate."

"I never would have guessed." It was hard to hide my sarcasm.

"Really?"

"Get real."

"I just wouldn't want you to feel uncomfortable with my not having much experience."

"You mean no experience." Score one for me. "Why is the glass all tinted so dark? I couldn't see you inside of here."

"That's why it's so dark — so nobody can see in when I'm driving."

"Why? Are you running from the police?" I joked.

"Do I look like a criminal?"

"More like a victim."

"Very funny. It was my father's idea. He didn't think it was safe for a woman to drive around in this city by herself. He's so old-fashioned, but that's the way he is, always worrying about me. You know how fathers worry about their ... " She let the sentence trail off to a painful and embarrassing silence.

"No, I don't know how it is."

She blushed. "I have some interesting news for you."

I felt a chill travel up my spine and dug my fingernails into the seat. What news could she possibly have that would be good?

"But I don't want you to discuss it with your sisters yet."

"Why not?" Now I was becoming really concerned.

"I want to wait until we know more. I don't want to get their hopes up if nothing comes of it."

"So it's okay to get my hopes up?"

"No, no, I didn't mean that. It's just that you're old enough to understand. Sometimes I have to remind myself just how young you really are. You act more like seventeen or eighteen."

Sometimes I feel a lot older than that. "So what's your news?"

"Will you keep it just between us for now?"

"It depends on the news. Maybe I'll tell Summer."

"I don't want you to do that without my permission."

"Your permission? I need your permission to tell something to my sister?"

"I have to make the decision if it's best for her to know at this time. You have to trust my professional training."

"And all your experience?" Score another point.

She didn't answer that one, just kept her eyes on the road. We drove along in angry silence for a minute till I realized I needed to hear the news more than she needed to tell me.

"Okay, so what's the news?"

"I was wrong. You're more like thirty-seven or thirty-eight." She turned off the radio and then knocked the air conditioner down a notch, making it much quieter in the car, so quiet I could almost hear my heart beating.

"You have an uncle."

This was the news? I started to snicker.

"Isn't that exciting?"

"Big news. We have plenty of uncles . . . and aunts and cousins and grandmas and you name it. Mom always had us call every bum she dragged home by names like that."

"No, you don't understand. I don't mean somebody you just call uncle, I mean a real uncle. Your mother's brother."

"My mother didn't have any brothers or sisters. She was an only child."

"An only adopted child," Joanne corrected.

That much was true. My mother had been adopted when she was little. Both her parents were dead now.

"Yeah, so what? She was the only kid they adopted."

"But you don't understand. Your mother had a brother, a natural brother!"

"You're wrong. If she had a brother she would have told us. She would have told me!"

"She would have if she knew."

"What do you mean, 'if she knew'?"

"Your mother was only three when she was adopted."

"Yeah, something like that. So what?"

"She would have been too young to remember any of that, so if her adoptive parents didn't tell her, and some don't, then she probably didn't know she had a brother."

"So you're saying —" I sank back in the leather seat and took two deep breaths. I felt scared and excited and upset all at once. "So you're saying . . . that we have a real uncle. Somebody who's related to us by blood?" What I didn't say was somebody who could maybe take care of us.

"That's what I'm saying."

"Where is he? Have you called him?"

"There are still some steps that have to be taken."

"What steps?" I asked suspiciously.

"Adoption records are sealed. It's very difficult to get information about people who have been adopted."

"What's so difficult about it? You just look in the computers and find out where he is and we give him a call . . . or maybe I should call, seeing as he's my uncle."

"It's not that easy. First off, they didn't have computers back then. We're talking more than thirty years ago. Sometimes the files aren't complete, and besides, privacy laws limit what I can find out."

"I don't understand. What has privacy got to do with any of this?"

"When somebody like your uncle, or your mother, are adopted, the adoptive parents have certain rights to make sure that the natural family doesn't interfere with their lives."

"Interfere! How can we interfere if he's our uncle?" I practically yelled.

"I know that must be hard to understand," Joanne said quietly.

"Of course it's hard to understand because it's stupid!"

"Lots of rules are stupid — I've learned that working here — but we have to be patient. I've found out some things and I'm checking the rest. Have a little faith in me."

"And all your experience?" I snarled. Joanne didn't answer, but I saw her expression change and I wanted to swallow back my words. None of this was her fault. She was just so easy to take shots at.

"We're pretty late. I hope Summer will understand," Joanne said.

"Summer never minds waiting. She's probably made friends with the trees and the flowers."

"I bet she'd try," Joanne chuckled. "Do you want to know what I've found out about your uncle?"

I wanted to know, but there was a battle going on between my curiosity and my pride. Curiosity won out. "Sure, I guess so."

"Your mother and her brother were taken away from their mother when they were two and seven. Their mother — your grandmother — fought through the courts for almost a year, but in the end she lost all rights to them. They were put up for adoption and placed in two different families. Your mother was three years old and your uncle was eight. I don't know why they didn't try to keep them together. Your mother would have been too young to remember her brother, but he probably remembers her. Your mother's real name was Ruby."

"Ruby? Her name was Rebecca, Becky to her friends. Are you sure?"

"Very sure. Sometimes the adopting parents give the child a new name."

"But wouldn't that be hard, being Ruby one day and Rebecca the next?"

"Very. I've heard of cases where children as old as ten were forced to take on a new name."

"That's awful. Even if you didn't like your name it's still yours."

"You're not so crazy about your name, are you Sky?"

"Would you be if you were called Sky?"

"I don't know. There must be some real advantages to being so unique."

"Like what?"

"For one thing, I imagine you've never been in a class where there were two Skys and the teacher got you confused."

"That's for sure," I said, chuckling.

"And nobody ever accused you of having a boring name — like Joanne."

"Boring would be okay. You know how tired I get of all the Sky jokes? Sometimes I'd like to be a Joanne, or Heather, or Rachel or Michelle or Melissa."

"I guess you're right. Let me tell you the rest of the information. Your uncle's name was Brian, and the family name, their last name, was Cole."

"Cole. Ruby Cole was my mother's real name?"

"Yes. So Brian was adopted at the same time as your mother, but into a different family. His new parents lived in this city. That's why I'm so excited. It means there's a good chance he still lives right here."

"But you don't know?"

"Not much more than what I've told you. We'll try our best to find him. I just have a feeling he's still here in the city."

"Or dead or in Alaska or maybe even in jail," I said.

"Well, I guess that's possible, but I'm just so hopeful we'll find him. I'm all ready to start the search."

"How do you do that?" I envisioned a new roll of red tape.

"We might have to take out a newspaper advertisement."

"Come on, you must be joking."

"No," she replied, shaking her head. "Sometimes we resort to that, but I'm hoping he's listed with the Adoption Disclosure Bureau."

"Adoption Disclosure —?"

"Bureau. Once adoptees turn eighteen they can put their names on a special list, and if other family members put their names there as well, then they're connected."

"And that actually happens sometimes?" It seemed like trying to find a needle in a haystack to me.

"I've been told it does, but I haven't been around long enough to have actually seen it take place. Look! There's Summer, up there on the porch." Joanne pulled the car over and came to a stop.

Summer was sitting on the steps of the foster home. She was wearing a flowery dress and her long blond hair was tucked up under a straw hat. On her lap was a cat and beside her sat a woman rocking in a chair. Summer saw us and waved. She gently handed the cat to the woman, raced down the steps — and then came to an abrupt stop. She bounded back up the stairs and gave the woman a kiss on the cheek. That was just like Summer.

"Joanne."

"Yes?"

"I think we should just keep this between us for now, okay?"

"I think you're right, Sky, I think you're right."

Summer skipped across the lawn, a smile plastered across her face. She opened the back door and climbed in.

"Hi, Sky," she said cheerfully. She leaned over the seat and gave me a kiss. "Hi, Joanne. Isn't it a lovely day?"

I chuckled to myself. "Lovely" was Summer's word of the month.

"It is nice. Sorry we kept you waiting so long. It's all my fault."

"What do you mean?"

"We were late," Joanne explained.

"You were?"

I turned around to face her. "About forty-five minutes. Didn't you notice?"

"No, I guess I didn't. It's such a lovely evening and I was just talking and listening and watching —"

"And day-dreaming." I turned around in my seat to face her.

"Yeah, I guess so," she answered, smiling. Her brow furrowed into a worried look.

"What's wrong, Summer?" I asked in alarm.

"Nothing."

"Then what's with the look?"

"It's just . . . you look really tired, that's all."

"I'm okay. It's probably because I don't have any makeup on," I lied. I looked tired because I was tired. I was only getting a few hours sleep each night. I laid awake in my bed for hours, staring at the ceiling and trying not to think so that my mind could slow down enough to let me drift off to sleep. I closed my eyes and listened to Joanne and Summer chatter away. A few seconds of sleep wouldn't hurt.

"How much farther is it?" I heard Summer ask.

"We're here," she answered. I opened my eyes as the car pulled over to the side of the road.

We climbed out and the locks clicked shut before we could even close the doors. I looked at Joanne.

"Automatic locks," she explained.

We all closed our doors and then jumped as the car beeped loudly.

"I just activated the alarm. Come on, ladies."

I fell in step behind Joanne, looking around as we walked. Weeds grew in the cracks in the sidewalk. The other cars on the street were night-and-day different from the one we'd driven up in. They were all older and some were pretty rusty. One car was up on blocks with all the wheels missing. Most of the houses were tidy, but a few were run down.

Joanne walked up to a tiny little bungalow, all scrubbed and freshly painted. The lawn was a healthy green and had just been cut. There were flowerbeds along the house, all neatly tended. A playhouse with a bright orange slide peeked over top of the backyard fence.

"It looks just like a dollhouse," Summer commented excitedly.

"And not much bigger," I replied, trying to give Summer a reality check.

We were halfway up the walk when the screen door flew open and banged against the house. Meadow came running to greet us. She must have been happy to see us because she let us hug her without drawing away. She even grunted a greeting. Debbie walked out onto the small front stoop,

Brooke in her arms. Why was she always carrying her around? The kid has legs, you know, I thought to myself. Brooke smiled and waved but didn't struggle to get down and run to me. She looked comfortable and happy in Debbie's arms. I should have felt good seeing her look so content, but instead I felt uneasy.

"Hello, everybody! Did you have any trouble finding us?" Debbie asked. She sounded genuinely glad to see us.

"No, your directions were good. I just got behind. I hope I didn't hold up dinner," Joanne said.

"No, not at all, no problem. Jack isn't even home from work yet. Please, come in." She held the door open with the arm that wasn't holding Brooke.

"Here, Brooky, come to me." I took Brooke from her and walked into the house.

The living room was tiny and the furniture seemed to be almost bursting out of the room. There were knickknacks everywhere, and one whole wall was covered with framed pictures of people, mostly kids.

"Why don't you girls settle in for a visit while I finish making supper."

"I'll help," Joanne volunteered.

"Debbie, who are all these people?" Summer asked, staring up at all the faces staring back at her.

"Oh, so you've noticed our wall of fame. Jack — that's my husband — and I come from really big families. He has seven brothers and sisters, and I'm the youngest of five girls, so there's always somebody having a baby. Hardly a day goes by without one or two nieces or nephews dropping by with their parents. That's why Jack built the playhouse."

"I thought the playhouse was for your kids," Summer said.

Debbie got all anxious looking. "We don't have any kids. It's not that we don't want them, or that we haven't been trying. It just hasn't happened yet. But, we're not giving up hope, no sirree." She paused and looked away from us and up at all the pictures. "Why don't you girls visit and we'll get supper ready. Jack should be home soon and he's always as hungry as a bear after working so hard all day."

Almost instantly Brooke grabbed me by the hand and dragged me in to see the room she and Meadow shared. Like the rest of the house, it was tiny. Between the two beds, placed side by side, the chest of drawers and a toy box, there was almost no space left to stand. It was crowded, but just like the living room, everything was neat and tidy. There were flowery curtains in the windows and posters on the walls. The beds were covered with quilts that matched the curtains, and a couple of stuffed animals sat perched on the pillows.

"Know which bed is mine?" Brooky looked like she was about to share a big secret.

"Of course I do. The one where Winslow is taking a nap," I answered, pointing to a plush white bear "sleeping" under the covers, with only his head peeking out. Brooke never went to bed or for a nap without Winslow, but since the accident, she seemed to need the bear even more.

Meadow had also told me about the difficulties Brooke was having at night. I wasn't the only one having trouble getting to sleep. Brooke needed to be rocked until she felt asleep and she was waking up in the middle of the night screaming and crying.

"HEEELLLOOO!" boomed a voice from the other room.

"It's Jacky Bear!" Brooke yelled and then ran, full tilt, out of the room. I got to the living room in time to see her being swept up into the arms of a man standing at the front door.

This man, who must be Jack, had long, straggly hair and he was wearing blue overalls covered with dirt and grime, and scuffed-up work boots. I couldn't believe they let people like him be foster parents.

Brooke squealed with delight as he lifted her high into the air and then lowered her onto his head. The uneasy feeling suddenly got stronger.

"I'm gonna wear you like a hat, just like a hat!" he said, laughing.

"Not a hat . . . not a hat . . . I'm Brooky!" she cried between bouts of laughter.

Meadow was completely ignoring the whole thing and sat staring at the TV. Jack put Brooke down and walked over to Meadow, stopping right between her and the set. She tilted her head slightly so she could still see the picture around him. Then he extended one foot backwards, and with the tip of his boot, clicked off the set. Meadow remained immobile.

"Well?" he asked.

"Well, what?" Meadow answered in a monotone.

"Are you going to say hello or am I going to have to stand here like a flamingo, on one leg, for the rest of the night?"

A smile barely creased the edges of her mouth. "Hi, Jack."

"Is that all?" he demanded.

She let out a big sigh. "How are you . . . did you have a good day?" she said mechanically.

"I'm fine, and I had a wonderful day. Thank you for asking." He giggled, then turned on the TV and got out of her way.

At that instant he caught sight of me standing in the doorway and he looked embarrassed. He might have even been blushing underneath all the dirt on his face, but it was hard to tell.

"You must be Sky . . . and you think I'm some kind of total idiot."

"Yeah, I'm Sky," was the only answer I gave, although he was right on both counts.

He came over and shook my hand. Brooke was at his side, asking to be a hat again. "Pleased to meet you, Sky. It's been just a joy having your little sisters around." He smiled and looked over at Meadow. "Although Meadow just keeps talking up a storm, she does."

Meadow smiled, a little, but there was no other reaction and she continued to watch her show.

"Debbie and I are so glad that the rest of you girls could join us for dinner."

"Yeah, sure."

"I wonder what we're having? Meadow, you and Brooke got to choose didn't you?" Jack asked.

She turned toward us and nodded ever so slightly.

"I'd ask her what we're having, but I wouldn't want to risk getting between her and the television again."

Meadow chuckled softly.

"Jack!" Debbie called out as she came out of the kitchen. She gave him a kiss on the cheek. "I see you've met Sky already. Summer is in the kitchen helping us with supper. You better get moving and wash up."

"I would, but I seem to have this thing attached to my leg!" Brooke was sitting on his foot, holding on tightly to his leg with both hands. He hobbled across the room with Brooke chuckling the whole way.

Summer and Joanne came out of the kitchen to see what all the laughing was about. They were wearing matching aprons. Joanne smiled brightly and Summer joined in the laughter. Brooke looked happy. And Meadow was so content she almost cracked a full smile. It should have made me happy to see they were doing okay, but it didn't. I felt worried, and somehow, scared.

* * * *

"Thank you for the lovely dinner," Summer said.

"It was our pleasure. Besides, you helped finish the pies," Debbie answered.

"Wasn't dinner good, Sky?" Summer asked.

"Yeah, sure. It was okay."

I hadn't really paid much attention to the meal. Half the time my mind had drifted off, thinking about this uncle we had somewhere and what that all might mean. Probably it meant nothing and there was no point in wasting even a minute thinking about it. The rest of the time I'd been watching how these people treated the girls. Everything seemed so nice. I thought about what it would be like to live in a house like this, with people like that. And then I wondered if maybe they'd want Summer to come and live with them, too — they seemed to like her. It was a tiny house and there might be room for one more kid — but not for two. I felt a gripping pressure in my chest like somebody had suddenly put their arms around me and was squeezing me tight.

"Why don't you girls go off and visit while we clean up the dishes and get dessert ready," Debbie said.

The chair legs scraped against the floor and we all bumped together trying to escape from the table. There wasn't nearly enough space for seven people around that tiny table. In the scramble Brooke toppled over and banged her head against something. She started wailing. I went to help her, but before I could get there Jack picked her up.

"Are you okay, Angel?" he asked. "Let me make sure my little angel isn't hurt."

"She's not your angel!" I snapped.

"I was just using a pet name," Jack explained over Brooke's screams.

"She isn't your pet and her name isn't Angel! It's Brooke, and that's what she should be called!" I shouted.

Brooke cried even louder in response to my raised voice.

"We have to talk," Joanne interjected.

Debbie quickly came over to Jack. "It's okay, Brooke, come to Mommy."

"What did you say?" I glared at her.

Brooke pressed herself against Debbie and wrapped her arms around her.

"You're not her mother and you'll never be her mother!" I screamed as I ran across the room and out the front door.

Chapter 3

"Ever think about getting air-conditioning for this thing?" I swept the back of my hand against my forehead to wipe away the sweat.

"Ever thought about how much money that would cost?" Ed replied.

Ed was a volunteer driver for the child-welfare agency. He took kids like me to and from appointments and visits and things. Ed had been my driver for almost all my visits the last five weeks.

"Besides, it isn't even that hot in here. I'm not sweating at all," he continued.

From where I sat in the passenger seat, I could see he was telling the truth. He wasn't sweating. I guess I was more nervous than I thought.

"I betcha it's a heck of a lot cooler in the trunk, though. Want me to pull over?"

"I'll pass on that, Ed." I laughed.

I liked Ed. He'd told me, the first time I'd tried to give him a hard time, that he was too old to take any guff from anybody. Ed was wearing stretchy peach-colored pants, held up by a white belt, an orange shirt with a crest of a little alligator swinging a golf club and a pair of fancy sneakers on his feet.

"Nice duds, Ed," I said sarcastically.

"Thought you'd like them. I dressed like this to impress you. How about you? I thought you'd at least find something without holes for the special meeting today."

"These are my best jeans with the best holes in them." I paused. "How do you know this meeting is special?"

"I heard a couple of the other social workers talking about it. They said that social worker of yours . . . what's her name?"

"Joanne."

"Yep. They were saying how much work she did to locate some fella."

"My uncle. At least they tell me he's my uncle."

"What do you mean by that? Either he is or he isn't."

"I guess he is. It's just I've never met him and we didn't even know we had an uncle until three weeks ago."

"I'm telling you, things sure are confusing these days. Back when I was growing up people knew who was their uncle and who wasn't. Things sure have changed. And speaking of change, how come you're in a different foster home?"

"Things didn't work out."

"Can you explain that to me?" Ed asked.

"We just didn't get along is all."

We didn't hit it off from the beginning. Then two nights ago I got into a big fight with my foster parents. It was about something so stupid that I can't even remember what started it. Finally I'd had enough and needed to go out so I could cool off. They told me I couldn't because it was against the rules. I left anyway and when I got back my bags were packed.

"They had too many rules," I said.

"Can you name me any place where there aren't rules?"

"These were stupid! Things like when I had to come in and when I had to go to bed, and there was a schedule for doing the dishes and —"

"Everybody's got to live by rules. Sooner you learn that the easier life will be."

Maybe he was right but I wasn't used to rules. My house never really had any. I certainly helped with the kids and worked around the place, but Mom treated me more like another adult than a kid. Being told what to do wasn't easy for me now.

"It's okay to be nervous," Ed said.

"I'm not nervous," I lied.

"Sure you aren't. I guess you're just twirling your hair like that 'cause you want to style it."

I pulled my hand away from my hair.

"Here we are," Ed said as he pulled the car up to the concourse outside the child-welfare office. It wasn't an old building but it was cold and angular, and didn't look like it had anybody's welfare at heart.

I got out and slammed the door.

"Hey!" Ed called out.

I turned around and leaned back into the window.

"I'll be back to get you in two hours. I'm going to hit a bucket of balls. Just wait here if I'm late. Okay?"

"Sure." I turned and started to walk away again.

"Hey!" he called out one more time and I came back to the car.

"Aren't you supposed to say something to me?"

I knew what he meant. Ed liked me to say thank you after a ride.

"Yeah, thanks . . . for dressing up so fancy for me."

Ed chuckled and then eased the car into traffic. He was a funny old bird but I liked him.

Inside the waiting area I searched the crowd for my sisters. They weren't there. I looked at my watch. I was twenty-five minutes early. The receptionist sat in the middle of the room, trying to deal with the phones as well as answer questions from the people swarming around her. There were so many hanging over top of her that I could barely see slivers of her. Every chair was filled. A couple, the woman holding a crying baby, were sitting in the corner arguing. Two kids were running around the room screaming, and their mother didn't seem to notice. Every face in the room was filled with one of two emotions, sadness or anger, no exceptions.

I made my way to a door at the far end with a big sign on the door: STAFF ONLY. Slowly I turned the handle and opened it, casting a glance back at the receptionist. She was still so besieged she wouldn't have noticed if somebody set the carpet on fire. I slipped inside and closed the door behind me.

I'd been in here a couple of times before, with Joanne. This was the area where she and all the other social workers had their desks. The desks were all thrown together in little clusters, separated by faded cloth partitions that reached less than halfway up to the ceiling and didn't do anything except pretend at privacy. The noisy confusion of the waiting room was replaced by the noise of an office. Telephones buzzed, one-sided conversations flowed over the partitions as people talked on the phones, voices called out as others tried to find things. People were too busy to notice me. Two women came toward me. They were both loaded down with arms full of papers and folders.

I didn't see how I could possibly pass by them in the narrow space between partitions. One looked directly at me and I could see in her face that she thought she should say something, but she didn't bother. At the last moment, like some sort of dance, they both turned sideways and glided past me.

Joanne had shown me a small area off to one side where they kept donuts and coffee. I wanted a donut but what I really needed was a coffee. My new foster parents wouldn't let me have any. They didn't even keep coffee or tea or pop in their house. If I'd known, I would have tried harder at the other foster home. Then again, it was just a matter of time before they kicked me out anyway. How did they expect me to follow all those rules, especially when most of them were stupid and didn't make any sense?

A couple more people walked by as I wandered down a corridor but nobody said anything. I turned a corner and came to a door. Maybe that was the coffee room. It was slightly open so I peeked inside. The room was long and narrow, just wide enough to allow people to squeeze behind some seats perched in front of a big glass window. It was the room behind the mirror! I stepped in and pulled the door closed behind me. The room was dark and the only light filtered in through the glass. From this side there was no mirror quality to the glass. It didn't send back my reflection. Instead it was like a window and I could clearly see the room we always used for our visits. On a ledge sat a series of small boxes — speakers.

A movement at the far end of the room caught my eye. The door opened and in rushed a harried-looking man in a tie. I ducked down so he wouldn't see me, but then remembered I was behind the mirror. He crossed over to one of the desks and started rummaging through the drawers. I stood up straighter now and watched him. I made a face at him. I stuck out my tongue and gestured with my hands. I laughed out loud and then clamped my hand over my mouth. Then it dawned on me that he couldn't hear me. And I couldn't hear him. He'd been rustling papers and slamming drawers and it was like watching a silent movie. There must be a control button somewhere to turn on the speakers.

The man seemed to have exhausted his search. He stood there mouthing words that were probably best not heard anyway. He walked toward the door, then stopped right in front of the mirror. My heart rose up into my throat. Our faces were only two feet apart. Had he seen me? With his fingers he started to comb his hair. Next he adjusted his tie. Then, grinning at himself, he stuck a finger into his mouth as if he was trying to dislodge a piece of food stuck between his teeth. He fished around for a few seconds, seemed satisfied and wiped his finger on his pants. He opened the door and left the room. Thank goodness! I was afraid of what other part of his body he might explore next.

A smile came to my face as a thought came to mind. If I could figure out how to turn on these speakers, I could sit in here, at least for the first part of the visit, and spy on Joanne and my sisters . . . and this man who was supposed to be our uncle. Somehow it seemed safer to see him for the first time from behind the glass.

Since Joanne first told me we had an uncle, I'd fantasized about what he might be like. Then when she told me they'd found him it got even worse. I'd tried to push the thoughts out of my head but they'd still come creeping back in, taking me by surprise when I was lying in bed at night. Thoughts about how he'd have a big house with a wife and kids of his own. And we'd meet and he'd be so happy he'd take us all to live with them. It sounded like something Summer would think up. Welcome to reality. People like Summer, and Mom as well, can afford to be that way because people like me are there to take care of them and the things that might cause trouble. I tried not to ever get my hopes too high — the higher they got the more it hurt when the fall came.

No sooner had I hatched my plot than the door opened again and Joanne walked in, followed by a man. I guess he was another one of her clients. Joanne told me she had about fifty different families she was working with, and that's why she was always late for everything. I didn't care about the other families. I just wondered how far behind she was today and how long she'd keep us waiting before she was through with this guy.

He was some piece of work. He towered over Joanne, but he wasn't heavy, just thin and hard looking, with stringy black hair hanging halfway down to his waist. One of those red and blue biker bandannas was tied around his head. He had a long dangly earring in one ear. A thick bushy mustache curled around his mouth and down the sides. Mirrored sunglasses, pointy-toed boots, well-worn jeans and a beaten-up black leather jacket with all sorts of zippers and things completed the outfit. On the back of the jacket was a gigantic eagle with the words ROAD WARRIOR in blood-red letters underneath. How could he wear leather stuff with the temperature around 12,000 degrees?

The only part of his face not covered by bandanna, sunglasses, mustache and stubble was his mouth, and it was scowling. I could understand why he was here. His kids were probably put into foster care at their own request, because they were scared of him.

I'd seen his kind before. Mom had some friends, and boyfriends, just like him. They act really cool and tough. Especially when they've got their buddies to back them or they're around women and kids. Put them under some real pressure and they scurry away like rodents.

He seemed to be getting really agitated, his hands flying around more and more. Even without the speakers I knew he was practically yelling. Tough guy, picking on Joanne. That took about as much guts as slapping a puppy.

I felt sorry for her. She didn't deserve this much grief, even though it was payback for some of the hassles she'd given me. It wasn't like she took my side when I had problems with that foster family. Either way, though, this didn't seem right.

As I watched, Joanne began retreating across the room. The jerk, his arms and mouth going a mile a minute, kept pace with her, moving forward each inch she moved back. I couldn't help thinking of a cat playing with a little frightened mouse, toying with it before swallowing it down whole.

What was he saying? My hands felt around the speaker and found a small switch on one side. I fumbled with it and jumped as the man's angry voice blared into the room.

"What do you mean I can't see the kids?"

"I don't think it would be appropriate for that to happen today," Joanne replied in a wavering voice.

"You get me all the way downtown on a day hotter than hell and tell me there's no visit? No way! I'm here and it's happening!" he yelled.

"No, it is not going to happen."

I had to hand it to her. Her voice was quivering but she wasn't giving in, not one bit. What a jerk. No wonder his kids were taken away and they didn't want to see him.

"You're doing this 'cause I'm an ex-con. I've done my time and I have the same rights as everybody else!"

"That has nothing to do with my decision."

He scowled even meaner and took a step closer. He had Joanne backed into a desk, and there was no place to go. He moved toward her, taking up the space she'd left and then leaned right over her. The cat was about to pounce for the kill.

"Leave her alone!" I hollered, shocking myself with my words, but of course they couldn't hear me, and he didn't move. He was going to hit her, I was sure of it. I'd seen it happen before. I flung open the door to the corridor. To my right was another door. It had to lead to the other office. I took a deep breath, flung the door wide open and jumped into the room. Joanne and the bully turned to me, their mouths open.

"Leave her alone ya big goof! Back off right now!" I yelled as I barreled across the room.

He took a small step backward and I felt a wave of relief. Then he turned and made a move toward me! The relief drained away as I realized he might hit me instead.

"Sky, I'm all right. It's okay." Joanne answered. She sounded shaken, but calm.

Okay? What did she mean?

Joanne's face was blank and impossible to read. I looked at the man. His mouth was twisted into a smirk and he was shaking his head.

"Sky, come over here."

I swallowed doubly hard. I was going to get it now. She'd give me heck for bursting in on her and then she'd want to know how I knew what was going on. And when she found out I was behind the glass she'd probably cancel our visit today and I wouldn't be able to see my sisters. I looked down at the floor as I walked toward them. I stopped a few feet short.

"Thank you, for what you tried to do," Joanne said.

I looked up in shock.

"We'll talk about it later, believe me. But not right now."

"Okay . . . you're welcome . . . I mean, I'm sorry . . . I mean, okay," I stammered.

Joanne turned to face the man. "I guess you get your way, Mr. Gray. Sky, I'd like you to meet your Uncle Cole."

Chapter 4

"This is my uncle?" I gasped. I really hadn't expected my dreams to come true, but I wasn't exactly expecting a nightmare either.

"This is one of my nieces?" he replied, his jaw practically dropping to the floor.

"There's even a family resemblance. You're both wearing the same expressions. Now why don't you two talk while I see if the girls are here yet." Joanne walked out of the room, leaving us alone to eyeball each other.

"Sky? What kinda name is Sky?" he muttered under his breath.

"Cole? What kinda name is Cole?" I snapped back and then remembered that it was my mother's, and his, surname before they were adopted.

He nodded and his mouth relaxed. He took off his shades and I was startled by the gentle blue eyes looking at me — eyes just like my mother's.

"Were you listening at the door?"

"Nope. Behind the mirror."

He turned to look at the glass. "One way, huh? They use them in police interrogation rooms . . . and jails."

"I guess you'd know all about that."

He looked taken aback, but only for a second. "Anybody else back there?"

"Just me. I snuck in."

A smile spread across his face. He folded his sunglasses and tucked them into one of the pockets of his jacket.

The door reopened and Summer bounded across the room and gave me a big hug. She released her grip and turned to Cole. Her expression didn't change a bit, a smile on her face, as always. Summer never cared what people looked like and she was probably the only kid in the world who wouldn't have been thrown by this guy's appearance.

"Uncle Cole!" she called out as she reached up and threw her arms around his neck.

Her surprise onslaught almost toppled him over. He looked shocked.

"I'm Summer." She released her grip.

"Summer? Sky? What are these two called," he pointed at Meadow and Brooke who stood wide-eyed at the door with Joanne, "Moonbeam and Spring?"

"Those are lovely names," Summer said, "but the big one's Meadow, and Brooke is the baby."

Meadow looked Cole up and down, a scowl spreading over her face. Then she strolled past all of us, her eyes on the ground, and plopped down by the basket of toys.

Brooke clung to Joanne's hand. She was partially hidden behind one of Joanne's legs, with Winslow clutched tightly under her other arm. The bear was wearing a beautiful necklace. Joanne shut the door behind her, and as the two of them walked across the room, Brooke worked at keeping Joanne between her and this man, although her eyes were fixed on him. Once they'd passed Cole she let go and settled down beside Meadow to play.

There was a heavy silence in the room. Now that we were all here, what came next? I looked at the others. With the exception of Brooke, who had her hands on a couple of toys but her eyes on our uncle, everybody else was examining their shoes.

"Maybe I should go and check my messages and give you all a little bit of privacy," Joanne suggested.

"No!" both he and I responded in unison.

Joanne looked a little embarrassed. "I guess you're right, both of you. This is a little uncomfortable for everybody. I'm not sure where to begin . . . does anybody have any questions?"

"Yeah, I do," I replied. "Why didn't you want the visit to take place today?"

"Yeah! You never did answer that for me! Why didn't you want me to see these kids?"

"You were going to stop the visit?" Summer sounded surprised.

"Yeah, she was trying to make me leave 'cause I've been in jail."

"That's not the reason!" Joanne protested. She was flustered.

"Then what is?" I asked.

"It's just . . . just —"

"What?" he demanded.

"I needed . . . well . . . more time to meet with you. I wanted to find out more about you before you met the kids." She glared at me. "Of course my plan didn't work out so well."

"What do you want to know?" Cole demanded.

"Well, I don't think we should talk in front of the children."

"I'm not one of the children. I have a right to know what's going on!" I argued.

"And you will, Sky. Even if I tried to keep things from you, I don't think I could be successful, but for now why don't you just visit and get to know each other. Okay?"

We all nodded but slipped into uneasy silence.

"How about if everybody pulls over some chairs and we sit and talk," Joanne proposed.

Soon the four of us were in a circle while Meadow and Brooke, still off to the side, played with the toys.

"So what do we talk about?" I asked.

"I don't know. Perhaps things you have in common."

"Like what?" I couldn't think of anything.

"Your mother for starters."

"Mom?"

"Your mother and Mr. Gray's sister. The most important thing you have in common."

A lump sat in my throat and a heaviness pressed against my chest. I wasn't sure I could talk to anybody about Mom, especially not some stranger, even if he was my uncle.

"I'd love to hear about when Mom was a little girl," Summer gushed.

Trust Summer to always say the opposite of what I wanted.

"Well, I don't know there's much to tell. Ruby and me were split up when I was seven. Last time I saw her I couldn't have been more than eight."

"Ruby?" Summer looked at me.

"Yeah, that was Mom's name before she was adopted," I answered in a whisper.

"What a lovely name! Ruby, like a jewel," Summer said with a dreamy look on her face.

Cole stared at Summer, his mouth slightly open, looking confused again. I was beginning to wonder if this was his usual expression.

"Don't let it bother you, she's just like that," I explained.

"It's just . . . it's just the way she was talkin' sort of reminded me of Ruby."

"Mom?" Summer beamed. "How?"

"She was always happy and smiling and —"

I nodded. "That sounds just like Mom. And Summer." Summer's smile grew even wider. She always reminded everybody of Mom. Sometimes that really bugged me. Lately I'd just been liking it.

"You mean she stayed that way . . . happy?" he asked. I could tell he was struggling for words.

"Yep. Almost always. No matter how much trouble we were in she always thought there'd be a way out and things happened for the best," Summer answered.

"That's . . . that's just like when . . . " he paused. We waited for him to start again but he didn't. His face looked pained and then he pulled out his sunglasses and slipped them on.

"Just like what?" Summer asked.

"Nothing." He scowled. "Just like nothing. I guess the people who took her were okay."

"Nanna and Poppy were very nice. I don't remember them very much though. Not as much as Sky would. I was only four or five when Nanna died and Poppy passed on just after that. Mom said he died of a broken heart because he couldn't live without her," Summer said.

"They were nice," I confirmed. "What about your parents?"

"Hah! They were lots of things but nice ain't one of them!"

"I guess they did some good things for you," Summer commented encouragingly.

"Only thing they done for me was finally setting me free. Kicked me out when I was fourteen."

"Fourteen! That's how old Sky is now," Summer replied.

"I'm almost fifteen."

"Where did you live after you were kicked out?" Summer asked.

"All sorts of places. Bounced around from one foster home to another till I was sixteen and then I took off."

Once again silence weighed heavily in the room. I squirmed in my seat and wondered how much longer before we could get going. Cole took one of his feet and rubbed the toe against the back of the other pant leg. Unlike the rest of him, his boots were shiny and new.

"Are you going to adopt us?" Summer asked.

"Adopt you! What makes you think I'm goin' to do that?" he boomed.

"You're our uncle. Isn't that why you came here today?"

"I was just curious, that's all. Nobody said nothin' about adopting no kids!"

"And it's not something to be taken lightly,"

Joanne added. "For a person to become eligible to adopt they must meet very high standards."

Standards way above this guy, I thought. That was so obvious there was no point even saying it.

"But that doesn't mean you can't have visits. After all, you live right here in the same city. It would be easy to arrange."

"That would be lovely!" There goes Summer again. Why can't she just keep her mouth shut?

He grunted and nodded ever so slightly, which I think meant he'd consider it. I wasn't so sure I would though. Maybe we shared a little blood but it wasn't like this was going to build to anything. Visits with him would be nothing more than a waste of a few hours a week.

"Our time is nearly up. I'd like the girls to visit on their own for a while. Could you join me, Mr. Gray, in my office? We have a few things to discuss."

"Like what?" he asked suspiciously.

"There are some monetary issues to be decided," Joanne said.

"You mean like money! I ain't got hardly none and —"

"No, we're not asking you for money," Joanne interrupted. "There is a lawsuit being pursued concerning the death of your sister."

Cole looked at his watch. "I don't know nothin' about any lawsuits and I got places to go."

"We really do need your input. It won't take

long and we're required to seek the advice of the next of kin. Besides, it's a large sum of money."

Cole sat up a little straighter. "Well," he said looking down at his watch again, "I guess I got a minute or so."

"You should say goodbye to your nieces. They'll probably be gone before we're through."

"Oh yeah, okay. Later, kids," he said, giving a nod and pointing one finger like a pistol.

Of course Summer would have none of this. She got up and gave him a goodbye hug and he blushed again.

"Wait a second," he said. "I got something maybe you girls would like." He reached into his back pocket and pulled out a battered old wallet that was attached to his belt by a thick chain. He opened it and removed a square piece of paper.

"Here," he said, thrusting it into my hand. It was an old, crinkled black-and-white photograph of a little boy and an even smaller girl.

"That's me and Ruby. You have it."

I'd never seen a picture of my mother so young. I didn't think she even had one. I stared at the little girl. She looked all happy. The little boy looked worried, like he knew what was going to happen next.

* * * *

Debbie picked up Brooke and Meadow. She was friendly to me and good to the girls and I felt badly about the way I'd treated her. It wasn't her fault Mom had died and Brooky liked her. I couldn't really put into words what I felt. I wanted to say something to her, but I didn't. After Summer left too I decided to wait outside for Ed. Cutting through the waiting room again, I wasn't surprised to see different people wearing the same expressions. Sadness and anger seemed so connected, either one could lead to the other.

A blast of hot air greeted me as I emerged into the bright light. I didn't like the heat but it felt good to get out of that building. Even the air in there was full of bad feelings.

I hurried down the steps and across the concrete plaza. Clusters of people, workers from the surrounding offices, gathered on benches to sip coffee or nibble on sandwiches or just to soak up some of the sun.

I saw Ed's car sitting at the curb with the four-way flashers blinking. As I got closer I realized Ed wasn't inside. Maybe we'd missed each other. I turned back and saw him. One of the good things about peach-colored pants is how they stand out in a crowd. I started trotting toward him, but stopped in my tracks. Ed was standing in front of a huge motorcycle, talking to a man. Even from the back there was no mistaking my uncle. What were they doing? What were they talking about?

"Hi! Sorry if I kept you waiting," Ed said as he saw me approach.

"No problem," I answered.

My uncle turned around and nodded.

"When I saw this bike I just had to come and have a look. You don't see an old beauty like this very often. Oh, where are my manners? Sky, this is —"

"You don't have to introduce us. We've met. This is my uncle."

"Your uncle!" Ed looked at me, then at Cole and back at me again. "Your uncle has quite a bike. Isn't it a beauty?"

I didn't know if beautiful was the right word, but it certainly was big and had lots of chrome. Ed started explaining all about the bike and used a bunch of words that made absolutely no sense to me about cc's and valve displacement and other nonsense. Cole nodded or added things to what Ed was saying. It was like they were talking a different language, one I didn't understand.

"We must be boring you," Ed said. He must have noticed the glaze over my eyes.

"Shouldn't we be going?"

"She has a point. Good to meet you." Ed and Cole shook hands.

"Good meeting you as well, Ed. Take it easy, man. You too, Sky."

Ed and I were halfway across the square when a deafening roar made it even difficult to think. Both of us turned around. Cole was astride his Harley, revving the engine.

"Purrs like a kitten, doesn't she?" Ed shouted, his voice was full of admiration.

"A big kitten." I said, but the words were drowned out.

Cole put the bike into gear and edged it forward. Pedestrians moved quickly out of his way. Every single person, sitting and standing, was watching him. He eased the bike down the wheelchair ramp, crossed the sidewalk and bumped down the curb and onto the road. The engine roared to life. I could feel the vibrations fill the air as he wove into traffic and passed cars as if they were standing still. He rounded the corner and disappeared, although the sound of the engine could still be heard for another few seconds.

We got into Ed's car and started driving.

"You sure know a lot about bikes."

"Fair amount. I used to spend my days riding one."

"You rode a motorcycle?"

"Yeah. Me. I wasn't born old, you know."

"I know, I know," I answered and then started giggling.

"What's so funny?"

"I was just picturing you riding a motorcycle . . . the wind blowing through your hair . . . wearing your peach pants."

"Very funny. I was usually wearing my uniform."

"What do you mean uniform?"

"That's what police officers wear."

"You were a cop?" I thought nothing else could shock me today.

"Thirty-five years. Some of them on motorcycles, and that's why I know a nice bike when I see one."

"Too bad that's the only nice thing about him."

"I don't know . . . you can't always judge a book by its cover."

"He had a pretty beat-up cover. You must have been looking so hard at the bike you didn't see the guy standing beside it! One look at him tells me all I need to know."

"And what's that?" Ed asked.

"That he's a punk. A biker. A gang member."

"You got part of it right. He is a biker, but he's no gang member. No gang colors or insignia on his jacket. He's an independent."

"So he's an independent punk, big deal. How does that make him okay?"

"Hold on now, girl. I didn't say anything about okay. I just said sometimes you can't tell by looking. Maybe he's a jerk and maybe he isn't. My gut didn't have time to decide."

"You mean you felt sick to your stomach when you were around him?" I laughed.

"Funny. You want to walk? It's only a few more miles. A cop learns to read people, you get a gut feeling about them. If you can't you won't make it, and I'm sitting here, wearing my peach-colored pants, having survived thirty-five years on the force. And I've seen hundreds of bikers. Jerks and punks, some of 'em. Others were a lot worse. Criminals, drug users, dealers, murderers. And some — not a lot, but some — were something different, better, or maybe had the potential to be something better. Sort of like diamonds in the rough."

I'd never heard Ed talk that much at once, or be so serious. I sat there unsure of what to say. My uncle a diamond in the rough? All I saw was the rough.

"And you think he could be one . . . a diamond?" I asked in amazement.

"Maybe . . . probably not . . . but maybe. Only know one thing for sure."

"What's that?"

"We're here." Ed stopped right in front of my foster home. I climbed out and closed the door behind me. I leaned back into the car.

"Hey, Ed, if you're so into bikes how come you drive this thing?"

"Only drive this sometimes. I have a classic. An old Indian. Ever been on the back of a bike before?"

"Nope."

"Scared?"

"Hah! I'm not scared of anything!"

"'Course you are. Only stupid people aren't afraid of anything. Maybe we'll find out the next time I drive you somewhere."

As Ed drove off, my hand went to my pocket and I pulled out the picture Cole had given us. My mother was about Brooke's age in the picture, younger than I'd ever seen her before. It was hard to believe that girl was my mother, but there was no mistaking the smile. And in her smile I could also see Summer and Brooky and even a bit of Meadow when she didn't know she was being watched.

My gaze then fell on the boy, my uncle. I thought about the sadness in his eyes and what he'd been through at such a young age. And I was shocked to see a bit of me, staring back.

Chapter 5

The bus pulled over and the brakes puffed it to a stop. The doors swung open and I climbed aboard.

"Hi," I said to the woman driver. "Is this the bus to Albert Street?"

"What number?" she asked.

I pulled the crumpled piece of paper out of my pocket.

"Four forty-eight."

"I turn down Delaney about twelve blocks before that. The bus down Albert doesn't run at this time of night."

I deposited my fare in the box. "I guess I'll have to walk the last part."

"Rough neighborhood for a young lady to be in alone at night."

"It's not that bad." What business was it of hers anyway?

"How would you know?"

"I've lived there all my life," I lied.

"Is that right? Then you must not be very smart."

"What do you mean?"

"Don't know many smart people who have to keep their own address on a piece of paper."

"We just moved to a new house. I meant I've lived in the area my whole life."

"Yeah, right," she answered, obviously not buying anything I was selling. "Take a seat."

I started to walk down the aisle.

"No, no, no! Right here, beside me. It's safer."

There were only six passengers. Three men, each in a separate seat, looked like they'd been sleeping on the streets. One woman, clutching a two-wheeled grocery cart filled to the brim with stuff, sat cackling and talking to herself. And two teenaged boys in the back seat. I didn't like the way they were leering at me. I sat down right across from the driver. Instinctively I reached up to fiddle with my hair and forced my hand back down to my side.

"How old are you?" she asked as the bus rocked away from the curb.

"Sixteen. I guess that'll be the last time I'll be able to say that. Tomorrow's my birthday and I'll be seventeen." It was always best to add details when you lie.

"Yeah, I guess if you're sixteen then seventeen does come next. Don't you think it's a little late to be out?"

"I'm just coming back from work."

"I see. And do your parents object to your being out — coming home from work — so late?"

"They worry. Especially my father. You know how fathers worry," I said, using Joanne's line. "But nobody said I shouldn't go."

That part wasn't a lie. Nobody said anything because nobody knew I was going. Not yet anyway, and maybe not at all. I'd waited until everybody had gone to bed for the night. That part was easy. In my foster home they all turned in by ten o'clock. Once I was sure they were all asleep I rolled an extra blanket and two pillows under the covers to make it look like I was asleep. Then I went through my bedroom window, and climbed down some latticework. It was a piece of cake. I'd snuck out a couple of times earlier in the week after everybody had gone to bed. I just needed to get out and walk and clear my head. I'd been able to get back in without anybody discovering I was gone. That was lucky. They weren't too happy about my being there . . . the foster father said I was a smart aleck . . . and I figured I was only one more thing away from having to move to a new place.

All week, since we'd first met Cole, I'd been playing around with ideas. At first I thought it was just plain stupid. There was no way he'd get involved, no way he could care for us and no way that they'd ever let us live with him.

Then I remembered how his ears had perked up when he first heard about the money. Maybe that would help him want to get involved. Even if he didn't know anything about kids, we'd get by fine. I was old enough to take care of myself and everybody else as well. It wasn't like I hadn't had enough practice. Mom gave me a lot of responsibility, most of the time because she wasn't responsible herself.

I was the one who checked the ads for specials and made the grocery lists. I made sure she remembered to take us for doctor and dentist's appointments and reminded her about Meet the Teacher Night. I took care of the kids sometimes for whole weekends at a time. What would be the difference doing it longer?

I'd spent a lot of time staring at the picture my uncle had given us. It was incredible to think that Mom could have known him, lived with him for the first couple of years of her life, and not even remember he existed. I thought about Brooke . . . if we were separated now she wouldn't even know who I was in a few years. As it was, she was getting too close to those foster parents.

I didn't like the way Brooke ran to Debbie at the end of our visits. Last week I had to call her back to get a goodbye hug. And Meadow was all excited about going to a baseball game with Jack. They were being drawn away from me. I could feel it. I couldn't just sit back and wait while my family vanished, bit by bit.

I'd been thinking about it for days. At night in bed, when I couldn't sleep, I'd try to weigh the possibilities. Finally, today at lunch, I reached a decision. Our best chance of staying together was with him. Maybe it was stupid but I had to try. It wasn't that I thought it was such a wonderful idea, but any idea looked pretty good when there didn't seem to be any other choices.

I looked him up in the phone book but he wasn't listed. I finally found his number, and address, with the information the foster parents keep. It wasn't easy to get it out of the desk drawer without being seen. I could have just asked them, but it was better that they didn't know I was interested in case they discovered I was missing and decided to send the police.

First I'd tried to reach him on the phone. I called every fifteen minutes from one in the afternoon until nine when they cut off our calls for the night. There was no answer, and it was important that I talk with him before the visit tomorrow, so I had no choice but to go and speak to him in person.

The bus stopped. My stomach gurgled. I always get sick in buses and being so nervous tied the knot in my stomach even tighter.

"Here you go."

"What?" I felt a little disoriented.

"This is where you get off."

I started down the steps. "Which way do I go?"

"That way," she answered pointing directly at a house.

"But you said I'd have to walk twelve blocks when you turned on Delaney?"

"That's four forty-eight Albert Street."

"But, how could that be?"

"Oops, my mistake. I guess I just forgot to turn."

"But . . . why?"

"I got a kid about your age. She's fourteen . . . so I guess she's a little younger than you," she said with a knowing smile.

"Yeah, a little," I acknowledged, feeling bad about lying to somebody who had done me a favor.

"And I wouldn't want her to walk these streets alone at night."

"Will you get in trouble for doing this?"

"Nah. Who's going to complain?" The only passengers left on the bus were the three street people and the lady with the grocery cart. "They don't care where I go as long as they get to ride all night. Cheapest hotel in the city. One dollar for the night."

I nodded. "Um . . . I guess I should thank you."

"That's okay. You run up to the door and I'll wait until you're inside."

"You don't need to do that . . . besides, the door is around the side where you can't see it."

"I can see the front door just fine from up here," she answered.

"We don't use the front. That's just for special, you know, when we have company."

"Whatever you say, kid. Get inside where you're safe, that's all. I'll watch as long as I can."

I turned up the front path of the house. I wanted to look around to check things out but I couldn't. I had to keep my eyes straight ahead and walk up to "my" house. Within steps, trees and bushes overhanging the path blocked the light from the street lamps. It looked like a tunnel and at the far end was the front door. A small yellow porch light above it cast an eerie glow.

Looking back I could see the bus still sitting there, waiting, the driver peering out the open door and down the path. I waved to her. She didn't wave back. I guess she couldn't see me, in the dark between the two points of light. Still she waited.

I was struck by the thought that I could just turn around and get back on the bus. I'm sure she'd take me someplace safe where I could get back to the foster home. I felt a moment of indecision. Part of me wanted to just give up this idea. After all it was a stupid one anyway. What was the point in chasing something that wasn't even possible? I was getting my hopes up again just to be let down.

Then the decision was made for me. The bus **groaned and I saw the door disappear and the lit** windows roll past until it was gone. I swallowed hard and walked up to the house.

It was a gigantic old house. A large wooden porch wrapped around the whole front and disappeared down one side. Gingerbread followed the roofline, although one piece was hanging down. Some of the spindles were missing from the porch railing, and paint was peeling off everywhere.

I was reassured to see lights shining out top floor windows. He must have got home between the time of my last phone call and now. Then again, maybe not. Next to the door were six different doorbells, slightly lit up. Beside each was a small space for a name, written in pen. Five of them had names. They were smeared and difficult to read but none of the names were Gray. The sixth was blank. Was this his apartment?

I pushed that buzzer and listened closely. I could hear it ring, somewhere up behind the closed front door. No response, just silence. I rang it again, this time much longer. Still no answer.

I tilted my watch until enough light hit the dial that I could read it: 11:35. Where was he? When would he be back? Was this even his place? How long should I wait? I didn't know, but I knew I had to stay.

My eyes followed the length of the porch. In the far corner stood a table littered with beer bottles and cigarette butts. Around it were four big wooden chairs with arm rests and high backs. I removed two empties from the arm of one chair and put them on the table. I held my breath as I moved a glass ashtray overflowing with smelly, yellowed butts. Yuck, how disgusting! I couldn't understand why people smoked, although I'd seen people do all kinds of stupid things. I pulled the chair away from the table, cringing as it scraped loudly against the wooden floorboards. I moved it nearer the front door and plopped down on the seat. Even though it was a warm summer night I felt a chill and drew my knees up to my chest, hugging them tight.

* * * *

I startled out of my sleep, unaware of where I was for a few seconds. The sound that woke me, an engine, faded to a gurgling and stopped. Silence. I remained motionless and listened. Nothing.

Then I heard footsteps. Shoes on concrete. They were coming from behind me. I braced myself as they hit against wood. I could feel them vibrating up through the chair. I wanted to turn around and look, but instead I drew myself deeper into the high back of the old chair.

A dark shadow passed by me.

"Cole?" I whispered.

"What the —!" he yelled as he spun around. A brown paper bag left his arms and flew across the porch. It landed with a loud thud, followed by a hissing sound.

"It's me, Sky!" I screamed back.

"You . . . what do ya think you're doing sneaking up on a fella?"

"Sorry . . . I didn't mean to scare you."

"I ain't ascared of nothing!"

"Please stop yelling at me," I pleaded, "you're scaring me!"

"Who's . . . yelling?" he asked, lowering his voice. "What are you doing here?"

"I need to talk to you."

"In the middle of the night?"

"I had to see you before tomorrow's visit."

"Visit?"

"Yeah. Tomorrow at the child-welfare office. You don't remember?"

"'Course I do. Just wasn't sure I was goin' to be able to make it. I was goin' to call."

I didn't believe him. He'd forgotten.

"Shoot!" he said, bending down to pick up the bag he'd dropped. He pulled out a six-pack. At least one of the cans was leaking and beer ran down the side of the cans and onto the porch. He turned the bag upside down. A package of pretzels dropped out, washed along by the wave of beer splashing onto the wooden floor.

"What a waste," he said, shaking his head. He looked up at me. "They let foster kids out at two in the morning?"

"No one said a word."

"Snuck out, huh?"

"Yep."

He chuckled. "Done that a few times myself. Bedroom window or back door?"

"Window," I answered, wondering how he'd know to even ask.

"That's better. Chance they won't even notice if you get back before morning."

"I don't care if they do find out," I lied. "Worst they'll do is send me to live with another set of strangers."

"How many homes you been in?"

"Counting the one I'm in now . . . three."

"Thirty-seven," he said.

"Thirty-seven what?"

"That's how many foster homes I was in from the time I was fourteen until I finally left when I was sixteen."

"How could you even remember them all?"

"I don't remember the people or places. Some of them I was only in for one or two nights, but I'll never forget the number. Thirty-seven. It's my lucky number. Come on," he ordered as he turned and started walking.

I jumped up off the chair. He used a key to open the front door and we walked down a dark corridor that smelled of old wood, stale tobacco and urine. As we passed one of the rooms, I heard pulsing music and two people arguing. I paused.

"Coming in?" He was standing at the end of the hall, holding open a door. He walked in. It was dark and I stopped just inside. A light came on. I looked around. There were newspapers and beer cans and clothes scattered everywhere. In one corner was an unmade bed, while in another a small fridge stood on a counter piled high with unwashed dishes that overflowed from a small sink. This was the kitchen. A portable CD player sat on a coffee table in front of a chesterfield. One of the arms was ripped and the stuffing peeked out.

I looked up at Cole who was looking at me and I felt a rush of fear. What was I doing here? Maybe he was my uncle, but I hardly knew anything about him and the little I did wasn't good. It was the middle of the night and nobody even knew I was here.

"Real fancy, ain't it?"

"It's —"

"A garbage pit."

"Well . . . the boom box is nice," I said pointing to the stereo.

"Only thing in here that's mine . . . the rest of the stuff came with the room." He had a foot up on a kitchen chair and was wiping beer off one of his boots with a rag.

"What is it you wanna talk about?"

He wasn't wasting any time. I sat down on the arm of the chesterfield. "I have a proposal," I said, using the words I'd been rehearsing in my head. "Proposal. You want to marry me?" He laughed.

"A deal. I have a deal," I stammered.

"Let's hear it." He took off his jacket and hung it on the back of a chair.

I was shocked to see his arms. They were covered with tattoos from shoulders to his wrists.

"You like my artwork?"

I was embarrassed I'd been caught staring. "Um, they're nice."

"What's the deal?"

"I want you to adopt us."

"Yeah, right."

"Let me explain what's in it for you."

"I know what's in it for me. Four kids!"

"And a lot of money."

"Money?"

"Yeah, when the lawsuit is settled. Our lawyer said he doesn't think it'll be much longer. He said the settlement would be big."

"Joanne said the money will be tied up tight in some trust fund thing. Nobody can see none of it until the four of you are eighteen."

"It won't be all tied up. And if you're our guardian, you'll be able to decide what happens to the money."

He stopped scowling. He picked up a chair and placed it right in front of me. "What makes you think I want your bucks?"

"People always want money, whether it's theirs or not," I answered.

"So you think I'd do it for the money do you?"

I didn't answer. It was too obvious to put into words.

"If you adopted us then you'd be in charge of the trust fund. You'd decide where it should be spent. Things like for a house or transportation and food . . . or a new Harley."

"I don't know nothing about looking after kids."

"You don't have to! I'll take care of everything. All you have to do is be around enough so we get left alone."

"You're just a kid yourself. What makes you think you can look after things?"

"I'm no kid. I'm fourteen, and I've been taking care of my sisters for years."

"What about my sister?"

I paused to think before answering. "She was there. It's just that she trusted me a lot and left me to do things . . . you know, it's hard when you're a single parent."

Cole got up from the chair and walked over to the counter. He pulled one of the beers free from the rings and opened it. The beer fizzed out and he put the can to his mouth to capture the liquid before it escaped. He took a long, long drink, his Adam's apple going up and down. When he finished Cole sighed, crushed the can in his hand, and tossed the crumpled container onto the counter.

"So you're just goin' to let me have the money."

"No, not all of it, but enough to keep you happy for the next seventeen months."

"Why seventeen months?"

"I turn sixteen. Then I can become my sisters' guardian myself. We won't need you anymore."

Cole's brow furrowed. "You think they'll let a sixteen-year-old take care of her three little sisters? Doesn't sound right to me."

"Of course they will . . . I'm sure of it," I said, hoping I sounded surer than I felt.

He stood there nodding and I could tell he was thinking about what to say next. "Why do you need me at all? Why don't you just wait out the time and then take care of it yourself. Seventeen months ain't much time, believe me."

"It's too long. Besides, the only reason they might let me have them when I was sixteen was if I was already taking care of them and you took off. And I'm scared that if I don't get them soon something bad is going to happen."

"Like what?" he asked.

"Like they'll be adopted." I looked down at the ground. "And we'll be separated."

"That stinks!" he thundered as he slammed his fist against the counter, making dishes rattle and jangle.

I jumped off the arm of the chesterfield.

"Kids need to be together . . . stay as a family." He stopped and looked up at me. "Who's kidding who? We's wasting our time even talkin' about this. Ain't no way in the world they're ever goin' to let me adopt nobody. Never."

"My lawyer says we have a chance," I replied.

"Who's this guy anyway?"

"He was appointed to represent us, to make sure the courts get to hear what we want. He told me the judges always look at family first, he told me we had a chance, he told me —"

"Yeah, and my last lawyer told me I'd be found innocent and all that got me was fourteen months plus time already served!" He walked over and grabbed his jacket. "Come on, you gotta get home. Ever been on a bike before?"

Chapter 6

"Are you okay, Sky?" Summer asked.

Her question interrupted my thoughts. "Yeah, sure. I guess I just hoped he'd be here."

"He may still show up."

Cole hadn't said no to my plan last night, but he hadn't said yes either. I guess his not being here was his answer.

"Where are those nieces of mine?" Cole drawled as he strode into the room. So money could make a difference. I smirked.

Joanne trailed behind him, looking exasperated. Cole was expecting Summer's assault this time and hugged her back.

He looked at me. "Come on, ain't my oldest niece gonna give me a hug?"

I hesitated. The girls and Joanne were waiting

to see what I was going to do. I could tell from Cole's expression he was enjoying putting me on the spot. I wrapped my arms stiffly around him.

"What are the other two called?" he whispered in my ear as he held me close.

I released my grip and turned away. "Meadow, Brooke, come see your Uncle Cole."

Meadow made a face at me, and then turned her attention back to what she was playing with. Brooke stared at me and then at Cole. She looked scared.

"Don't be shy! Come and see your uncle!" he thundered. Before anybody could say or do anything he bent down and scooped Brooke up in his arms. She started crying at the top of her lungs.

"Don't worry! I gotta way with kids!" he yelled above her screams.

"A bad way," I muttered so nobody could hear me.

"It's okay, Meadow, don't cry," he bellowed.

"That's Brooke," Summer corrected.

"I knew that . . . just got confused a little . . . no problem. Don't cry, Brooke, be nice to Uncle Cole."

"Here, let me take her," I offered.

"Nope! She better get used to having her uncle around."

Cole took a seat and put Brooke on his lap, facing me. This seemed to have a calming effect. She stopped crying.

"Told you I have a way with kids!"

"I'm glad you came today, although I am a bit surprised," Joanne commented.

"What's so surprising 'bout a man wantin' to see his nieces?"

"Nothing. It's just that I've been trying to get hold of you all week. I've called dozens of times each day, right up until fairly late at night."

"Don't understand that. I'm almost always home in the evening. You must've been callin' the wrong number or something."

"I . . . don't think so . . . I guess I better check before you leave today," Joanne said in confusion.

"Hey, Sky, I saw your buddy, Ed, outside. He told me he brought you here today on the back of his bike. Was that your first time on a cycle?" He winked.

"No. Once before." I had to fight to keep a smile off my face.

It had been less than eight hours since he'd dropped me half a block from the foster house. He didn't want to get any closer because the noise from the bike might have woken somebody up. My ears were still hearing fuzzy static as I finally climbed into bed last night. Luckily I'd got back in without anybody even missing me.

"So when do I get to adopt my nieces?"

"When do you what?" Joanne eyes opened wide. This was going to get interesting now.

"Adopt my nieces."

Summer shrieked and threw her arms around

him. Brooke started to cry again and even Meadow stopped playing. Then everybody started talking at once. Joanne, looking worried, tried to interrupt our conversation, but we just ignored her. She was probably used to people ignoring her.

"Excuse me!" Joanne finally yelled and except for Brooke, everybody fell silent and looked at her. "Thank you. You can't be serious, Mr. Gray."

"Why! Are you saying nobody would want to adopt us?"

"Of course not, Sky, that's not what I meant at all," she replied all aflutter.

"Then what are you sayin'?" he demanded as he rose to his feet and took a few steps toward Joanne. With Brooke still in his arms he looked more comical than threatening, but Joanne still backed away.

"I'm just saying adoption is a very serious matter."

"Ain't nobody laughin' here . . . unless it's you laughin' at me 'cause you don't think I could be a good parent!"

"I didn't say you couldn't be," she apologized, looking more and more flustered with each passing second.

"So you're saying he would be a good parent?" I said, pouncing on her indecision.

"No!" she yelled, and then she must have remembered who was supposed to be calm and in control. "I mean, no, I'm not saying that either."

"Then what exactly are you saying? Spit it out!" Cole was practically leaning over her.

"It's a complicated process. You can't just walk in here and say you're going to adopt the girls —"

"Yeah I know. I figured I'd have to sign some papers or something. Go get 'em and I'll sign 'em right now." Cole sat down again and placed Brooke back on his knee.

"You don't understand!"

"Then you ain't explaining it right. I ain't stupid, you know!"

"For one thing we're still trying to locate the girls' fathers. They would have first rights to take their children."

"And I bet you've had a lot of luck finding them, haven't you?" I had her there.

"Well . . . we're still looking."

"But our lawyer told me we could be with our uncle on an interim basis while you were looking," I said.

"What's interim mean?" Summer asked.

"It means, like, for a while, until something permanent happens," I explained.

Cole winked at me and I couldn't help but smile. He took a seat again.

"You can investigate all you want. All you gotta know is we're blood and blood should be together. These girls don't need to be living with strangers. They need to be with family. I want to care for my nieces and they want their uncle to raise them. I know I'll be a good daddy to 'em. That's all there is to know. Case closed."

"Yeah, that's right!" I agreed.

"How soon before we can move in with our uncle?" Summer asked.

Meadow put down her toys and stood right beside us, nodding too.

"I understand how you girls feel," she started to say. How could somebody like her, driving in her daddy's BMW, ever know how I felt? "And I certainly am sympathetic to your feelings, it's just there are certain things that must be undertaken and these things take time."

"Aaaahhhh!" Cole screamed as he leaped to his feet again.

His outburst startled everybody. Joanne practically hit the wall she jumped back so far. He turned to face us, holding Brooke away from him at arm's length. She was dripping onto the floor and there was a gigantic wet spot on his lap where she'd been sitting.

"I'm all covered with —"

"Here, let me take her!" I rushed over to take Brooke. I wanted to stop him before he said or did anything to jeopardize what we were doing. He started to offer her to me and then stopped. He turned to Joanne.

"Accidents will happen . . . poor little thing got herself all excited about coming to live with her uncle. Can't blame the little darling. Anybody bring a change of clothes?"

"I'll go and check with her foster mother. She's in the waiting room." Joanne ran through the door.

"Here, you can take this now." Cole said as he handed Brooke to me, but I held her away from me as well. No point in three of us being covered in pee.

"One good thing about this," Cole said.

"What's that?"

"At least now, I'll never get their names confused again."

"What do you mean?"

"The one filled with water is Brooke," he said, pointing to the puddle on the floor.

* * * *

When I came out of the building a while later I wasn't surprised to see Cole standing beside Ed. He'd parked his bike beside Ed's. Cole climbed onto Ed's machine and started it up. It roared as he revved the engine. I stood slightly back, kept away by the waves of thundering sound, and watched them yell things back and forth into each other's ears. Once again people on the benches, chewing on their sandwiches or smoking their cigarettes, were all staring at the two men and their machines. They were the entertainment. Finally the engine faded and then gurgled to a halt. They both greeted me as I walked up.

"You should have seen your niece this morning. Climbed on my bike like she'd been doing it her whole life. Even leaned into the curves the right way, real relaxed, not tense at all. She's a natural!" Ed clapped me on the back.

"Do tell." Cole feigned surprise.

"Yep. Hard to believe it was her first time on a bike."

"You mean you'd never been on a bike before?" Cole enjoyed putting me on the spot.

"Like I told Ed, last week, I'd never been on a bike before." I'd answered the question without actually lying to Ed again. For some reason it bothered me to lie to him.

"She's a natural rider." Ed beamed. "You weren't scared at all were you?"

"Not a bit."

Ed drove slowly in the curb lane, so slowly cars were continually passing us. He took the curves gently and talked to me as we drove. That was a lot different than my first ride. Last night I was scared. I knew Cole had polished off at least one beer, and probably more, and he was racing through the streets, yelling at me to lean every time we rounded a corner. I thought he was deliberately trying to hit all the bumps.

"We need to talk," I said to Cole. "When's a good time to call you?"

"Isn't any good time, but the later you try the better the chance. 'Course you got to know the signal."

"What do you mean?"

"I only answer the phone if it rings the way I want it to."

"I don't understand."

"People I want to talk to know they have to let it ring three times, then hang up. Call back and let it ring two times and then hang up again. Call back and I pick it up. Otherwise I don't answer."

"Why wouldn't you just answer it?" I asked.

"Only want to talk to people I want to talk to. That's all."

"How long you been riding independent?" Ed asked, changing the subject abruptly.

"What makes you think I haven't always been?" Cole's tone suddenly seemed different and harder.

"Your jacket. There's a couple of places where the leather isn't as weathered. You've taken off emblems on the back and right front. Same shape, just bigger on the back." Ed's voice had changed as well. He was sounding like the cop he used to be. "How long you been independent?"

Cole didn't answer. He took his sunglasses out of his pocket, slipped them on and then climbed off of Ed's bike. He pulled the keys from the ignition and dropped them into Ed's hand. Ed was standing straight. I hadn't noticed before how tall and big he was. His expression was as cold and hard as Cole's. He didn't look like a friendly old man anymore. They stood and stared, eyeball to eyeball. Cole reached into his jacket and grabbed something.

"Here," he said, keys dangling from his hand. "Start mine."

Instantly the tension dissolved. Ed smiled and then slouched forward. The cop in him vanished.

"Thanks." He took the keys and climbed onto the Harley. He went to turn the keys, but Cole reached out and stopped him.

"Important thing ain't how long I've been independent but that I'm independent now."

Ed nodded. "I had no right to ask you, anyway. I guess I still think I'm a cop sometimes even though I've retired." He started up the engine and I retreated to a bench while they started yelling things into each other's ears again.

Chapter 7

"It's important for you to be back by five o'clock," Joanne said, for the second time.

"Yeah, don't worry, no problem," Cole answered. "Anybody gotta watch?"

"I do," I replied.

"I ain't never had no watch. I figure what difference does a few minutes make one way or another? I get where I'm going, sooner or later."

"I'll make sure we're back on time, Joanne."

"Thanks, Sky. It's important. There'll be three different drivers waiting here at five to take you all back to your foster placements."

"That would be some change, me keeping Ed waiting," I chuckled.

We walked out through the front doors. It was already a scorching day without a cloud in the sky.

Brooke was between Cole and Summer, and they were swinging her up in the air every few steps. She was laughing and screaming. Every time they swung her she pleaded for them to stop and when they did she begged them to do it again. I couldn't help smiling, but it felt strange to feel even a hint of happiness. This plan just might . . . I stopped myself before I went any further.

Brooke didn't fear Cole anymore. She'd become more comfortable with him in the six visits we'd had in the two weeks since he first told Joanne he wanted to adopt us. This was our first unsupervised outing. It was going to last the whole day. Joanne was nervous about it, but I had to admit he was doing a pretty good job of acting. He was really earning his money and I think he was starting to fool Joanne. Of course fooling Joanne didn't require Academy Award acting ability.

The agency was still searching for our fathers, but I knew they were looking for the wrong names in the wrong places and would never find them.

"There she is!" Cole announced, pointing at an old white Chevy parked at the curb. It had a big dent in the back door, and blotches of rust bubbled through the paint.

"We're going in that?" Meadow was so impressed she actually talked.

"Yeah, what'd ya think we were goin' to do, all climb on my bike?"

"It looks fine to me," Summer chipped in.

"Sky, could I have a word with you?" Joanne asked. "Privately."

I followed her as she walked away from the others who were climbing into the car. "I'm counting on you to keep an eye on everybody."

"Even my uncle?"

"No, I mean your sisters. I need you to watch them."

"But that sounds like something a mother would do and you keep telling me I'm not their mother." Score two points for me.

"But big sisters do watch their little sisters. Besides, I don't think you could relax even if you wanted to."

She was right about that. "My uncle is there to take care of everybody."

"Sky, I don't mean to say negative things about your uncle," Joanne began.

"Then don't!"

"I have no choice. You want me to be honest with you don't you? I'm sure you're aware the agency, and I, have some doubts about him."

"I don't care if you have doubts, he's our uncle!"

"I know, and nobody would ever stop you from visiting with him, but I don't know if he's suitable to care for four young children."

"Why? What's wrong with him?" We didn't have enough time for her to list all the possible concerns.

"Well, for one thing, do you know he has a criminal record?"

"I know. Remember the first meeting when you didn't want us to see him?"

"Of course, but did you know how lengthy it is?" Joanne questioned.

"Just because he's made mistakes in the past doesn't mean he can't be a good parent," I paused. "But I guess it depends."

"I'm glad to see you can still be objective about this, Sky. We're not trying to be unreasonable, it's just that sometimes what people did in the past indicates what they might do in the future."

"You're right, Joanne. I'd be scared if he's committed murder or something, or hurt a woman or child. If he's done any of those things then I don't think we should go and live with him."

"Well," Joanne said. "I looked at his record, as part of the review your uncle agreed to for the interim-care application, and he's never been involved in any of those types of crimes."

"That's good."

"But there are other considerations about his criminal record," she continued.

"Yeah, there should be. Like if he was still committing crimes all the time then he shouldn't be able to care for us. I'd only feel all right if he hadn't broken any laws for at least the last year or so. That would show he's changed. How long has it been?"

"Um . . . his last conviction was over eighteen months ago."

"So way more than a year. That's good news. What a relief!"

Of course none of this was either a relief or news to me. Ed had a friend of his run Cole on the police computer and he'd read me a list of all his offences. Ed said one of the advantages of being a cop, even a retired one, was you could get information. He'd made me promise not to tell anybody what he'd done.

I didn't really know if Cole hadn't committed a crime lately or if he just hadn't got caught. I did know that he certainly got caught enough in the past. His convictions started as soon as he was sixteen and spanned the continent. Ed had explained he probably had priors, other convictions before that age, but juvenile records were sealed after somebody turned sixteen unless there were really major crimes, like murder or kidnapping. His list of crimes was large but nothing like that.

His first offence was stealing a car and then taking off when the police tried to stop him. What followed were assorted thefts, breaking and entering into businesses, some drug and driving charges and fraud. Two of the charges were for driving while impaired. Like the man who'd killed Mom. I would have liked it better if this were something from his past, when he was young, but I was pretty sure he was impaired the night he drove me home.

Thank goodness he hadn't been drinking today. I made a point of smelling his breath when he gave us all a hug. I didn't want to drive with somebody who'd been drinking, although I didn't have much choice. Whether he'd been drinking or not we had to climb into the car and have this visit. I was just glad he'd saved me from having to deal with a bad situation. Maybe he was being responsible. More than likely, though, it was because it was ten o'clock in the morning and nobody drank that early — except an alcoholic.

The conversation was over so I got into the back seat. Brooke was in the middle between Meadow and me. Meadow had her nose buried in a comic book. Summer sat up front.

We waved goodbye to Joanne as Cole tried to start the car. The motor sputtered and groaned but didn't seem to want to catch. He tried again, and again. Finally it roared to life, a noxious cloud of thick blue smoke belching out the exhaust. It drifted back through the open windows and we all started to cough. It burned my eyes.

He put the car into gear and we left the cloud behind us. We'd only traveled a few car lengths when the engine died. We rolled to a stop and he cranked the engine again. A car behind us started to honk and Cole stuck one arm out of the open window and held it high. I couldn't see but I had a pretty good idea what he was signaling, and it wasn't a left-hand turn. Mercifully the engine caught again and we started sailing down the road.

"Where to? Where am I aiming this tank?"

"Head for Grover Avenue," I directed.

"Okay, boss," he answered as he made a fast turn at the corner. "What's there?"

"Wild Water World," Summer answered. "It's great, or at least the commercials I've seen are great. It's a water park. It has slides and a wave pool and a lazy river ride —"

"Whoa! I don't want to go to no water park!"

"But you said we should pick the spot, that you didn't care where we went!" Summer protested. "And they're really fun."

"Come on, I didn't even bring along a bathing suit or nothing."

"I brought one for you," Summer answered matter-of-factly.

"You did?"

"My foster father lent it to me. I brought a towel as well."

"I don't care, no water park, forget it!"

At that point Meadow, who as always seemed to be ignoring everything, put down her comic. She leaned forward and tapped him on the shoulder. "You said we could choose any place we wanted. We did. Either take us there or take us home. Keep your promise."

I saw him open his mouth to answer but then he clenched his jaw and the veins on his neck started to bulge out. He turned the car sharply at the next intersection. The tires squealed as we curved into the oncoming lanes of traffic as we rounded the corner. We traveled in silence for a few minutes. I didn't know if the last turn was bringing us to the water park or back to the child-welfare office. Nobody said anything. We just drove along.

"There it is!" Summer shouted, pointing out the front windshield.

On a hill a gigantic billboard announced we were close to Wild Water World. It featured pictures of people in their bathing suits playing on the water slides and in the pool.

Of course for me it wouldn't be much fun. I'd have to be on constant alert, watching over my sisters, making sure they were safe and not doing anything dangerous and that the water wasn't too deep and the slides weren't too high. You have to watch because accidents do happen and I was responsible for making sure nothing happened to them.

He turned into the entrance, a long driveway lined on both sides by flagpoles, their flags fluttering in the wind. Behind the fences I could see the wooden stairs and towers leading up to the water slides. There were small lineups at the top of each slide as people waited their turn. As he slowed down by the main gate, the car's engine died once again and we coasted to a stop. He muttered something under his breath and I was grateful he hadn't spoken any louder. He turned the key. The engine struggled to turn over, sputtered and then died. He tried it again. It didn't catch.

A car honked. I turned around and saw three cars lined up behind us. He tried the engine one more time, but it failed again. The honking started once more. This time the guy kept his hand on the horn for five or six seconds. I was almost grateful for the sound because it drowned out most of the things Cole was muttering.

"Come on, lady! Get that heap off the road!" somebody yelled.

With his long hair, Uncle Cole did look like a woman from behind. He was so intent on starting the car that he didn't seem to hear what was said, or if he did he didn't realize the insult was being hurled at him.

I looked back. Right behind us was a fancy red sports car. There were three or four guys, I couldn't see for sure, and two of them were leaning out of the windows.

He tried the engine again. It coughed and sputtered, coming so close to catching and then, nothing.

"Learn to drive, lady!"

Cole stopped. "What did he say?"

"Learn to drive, lady," Summer answered. "Before that I think it was something about getting our car off the road."

"Stupid broad!" came a third taunt.

I shuddered as I looked over my shoulder. Those guys were having a good laugh, screaming at us. Cole opened the door and climbed out of the vehicle. I looked at the red car as he started walking toward it. The car was the same, shiny and new and expensive, but the expressions on the occupants' faces were completely different now. What was he doing? I opened the back door and jumped out. Before I could even take a few steps he was standing right beside the open driver's window of the sports car.

"What was you saying?" he bellowed.

I couldn't hear any answer. I moved up closer. I could now see there were five of them in the car, and they were just teenagers.

"So your daddy let ya have his car today, did he?" Cole yelled.

Another answer I couldn't hear, although I saw the driver's lips move.

"Betcha he'll be pretty unhappy if it comes back all dented up!" Cole thumped the palm of his hand on the roof of the car.

The line of cars behind us continued to grow steadily. A crowd of people gathered on the sidewalk. I wanted us to get out of here, and quick. I rushed to Cole. The last thing we needed was for him to get into trouble today on this visit.

"Come on, we better get going," I said.

"Can't . . . got some manners to be teaching."

"Leave him alone! Please!" I pleaded.

His expression stayed as hard as steel.

"Please, Uncle Cole! Please, Uncle Cole!" It was the first time I'd called him uncle and the word caught in my throat as I said it.

He scowled at me for a few seconds and then his face softened. He took his hands off the ledge of the window and straightened up.

"Come on," he said, walking back to our car. I trailed happily after him.

"Thanks, Uncle Cole!" came a high-pitched taunt from over my shoulder. I stopped in my tracks as did Cole directly in front of me. He spun around and the look on his face was frightening. He bounded back to the car. He reached in, grabbed the driver and pulled him partially through the open window.

"It wasn't me! It wasn't me! I didn't say anything!" the driver screamed as he got dragged the rest of the way out of the window. He looked as scared as Cole looked scary.

"Then which one of them did?"

"Him! It was him!" the driver screamed, pointing to the guy in the passenger seat.

Cole tossed the driver aside as if he was a rag doll. He reached in through the window to get at the passenger, who was desperately leaning away from Cole's outstretched arms. Just as it seemed impossible for him to escape, the passenger door opened and the teen dropped to the pavement. Before Cole could react the guy scrambled to his feet and started running away at full speed. I was amazed at how fast he was moving.

Cole straightened up. "All of ya, out of the car!"

The three people in the back seat scrambled out the far door, keeping the car between them and Cole. The driver got off the ground and joined them.

Cole crooked a finger, indicating he wanted them to come over to where he was standing. They inched forward, bumping into each other as they came, then stopped a few feet away.

"Does anybody else have anything they want to say to me?"

They all shook their heads vigorously.

"Good, none of you look like you're smart enough to do two things at once, and I need you to do something. So you all agree you should be giving me a little help?"

"Yes, sir," one of them mumbled. The rest nodded their heads like those little ceramic dogs people sometimes have in the back window of their car.

"Good. Now you," he said, pointing to the driver. "Get in your daddy's car and turn it around so it's facing the right way . . . toward the exit. None of you is going to no Water World place today. And the rest of you, come with me. You're going to push my car to a parking spot. Anybody got any problems with that?"

They all shook their heads.

We got back into the car and the three boys started to push.

"There's a spot, right there!" Summer exclaimed, pointing to an opening not very far away.

"Nah! I want one of those spots, over there. Way over there!" he indicated the nearly empty lot at the far end of the parking area. "A valuable car like this you don't want to park beside other vehicles. You know, I wouldn't want nobody to bang the doors or nothin'."

We picked up speed as the boys continued to push. I looked back and saw the fourth join in. He'd parked his car and come to help his friends.

I heard the engine crank over and turned to see Cole trying to start the car once again. The motor sputtered and then blazed to life. He revved the engine and it roared. We slowed down and rolled to a stop. The four boys were ten feet back.

"Hey!" Cole yelled out the window. "Keep pushing!"

"But the car's working now," Summer protested.

"Yeah, but just 'cause it's working don't mean they should stop working. These guys need a little exercise for their bodies. So far all I know is that they know how to flap their gums." He leaned out the window. "Come on, move it, move it, move!" he yelled and they started pushing again.

They pushed for another dozen or so feet before he popped the car into gear and it squealed away, leaving a trail of rubber. I was pressed against my seat by the sudden acceleration. I recovered and looked through the rear window. The four boys littered the roadway. Cole roared with laughter as he pulled into the first available parking spot. He turned the car off.

"You know something, Summer, you was right. These water parks sure can be fun."

We got out of the car in time to see the little red sports car zip out the exit and away from the water park.

"Uncle Cole?" Summer asked.

"No more Uncle Cole! From now on it's just Cole! Just call me Cole."

"But you're our uncle," Summer objected.

"I know I'm your uncle, it's just that, I don't know, it seems wrong or something to call me that. Do I look like anybody's uncle?" he asked, gesturing to himself.

He had no argument from me. I only called him uncle in front of Joanne and it always left a bitter taste in my mouth.

"You don't want to be our uncle?"

"I didn't say that. It's just you heard the way that guy made fun of us."

"But he was a jerk," Summer said.

Everybody turned to her in shock. It wasn't like Summer to say anything bad about anybody. I was surprised she didn't tell us they were "lovely" boys. She looked embarrassed.

"Well, he wasn't nice," Summer explained.

"No, he was a jerk," I confirmed.

"Yeah, he was, but I bet he's one tired jerk. Probably ran all the way home," Cole chuckled.

"And through the front door, up the stairs and under his bed," I added.

"Then you want us to call you Cole?" Summer asked, sounding disappointed.

"No," Meadow said.

When you talk as little as Meadow does, people stop and listen if you open your mouth.

"No?" He looked astonished.

"No. We're calling you Uncle Cole."

He glared down at her. She stared back just as intently. He shrugged his shoulders and smiled weakly. "Call me Uncle Cole."

It really didn't matter to me because I was calling him Cole whether he liked it or not.

* * * *

We stood off to the side while he bought the admission tickets. We all filed in through the turnstile. A girl, not much older than me, chewing on a big wad of gum, sat on a stool just inside the gate stamping hands.

"What does MMM mean?"

"MMM? No, you're reading it upside down, Cole. It's WWW. Wild Water World. This lets you go in and out of the park all day."

Each one of us in turn got stamped. Cole reluctantly held out his hand. I couldn't understand his hesitation. It wasn't like he didn't have any marks anywhere on his body. Maybe he would have preferred a tiger or a cobra or something instead of just initials.

"Here's your bathing suit," Summer said, handing Cole a plastic bag. "We'll meet you back out here after we get changed."

He grunted out a reply. I watched him walk over to the change room marked Gents. I didn't think he qualified as a gent, but it was obviously a better choice than the door marked Ladies.

I was fascinated by how people reacted to Cole. They got out of his way, and while they sometimes turned to look at him as he passed, they always made sure that he didn't see them stare at him. People had been acting that way since we first got out of the car. Maybe it was just those who'd seen the fight out in front of the gate. Who was I kidding? I was sort of getting used to being around him, but before I'd met him I would have stared at somebody who looked like him. Stared and stayed out of his way.

"Come on, Sky, let's get going!" Summer called out as she and the others disappeared into the ladies change room.

We put on our suits and jammed our things into a locker. I pinned the key to my strap. Outside, Cole stood leaning against a post. He wasn't wearing his jacket or shirt anymore but he still had on his jeans, bandanna and boots. His chest and back were covered with a colorful assortment of tattoos too. They stood out even more in contrast to his skin. While his arms were tanned, his shoulders and chest were as white as a ghost. I don't think they'd ever seen the light of day.

"Why aren't you wearing the bathing suit?" Summer sounded disappointed.

"Bathing suit! I've seen bigger napkins! Did you see that thing? It's one of those little bikini jobs. Ain't no way I'd wear something like that even under my jeans."

"But they won't let you into the water without a bathing suit," Summer protested.

"Who said anything about going into the water?"

"But you'll miss all the fun!"

"I've already had my fun."

"All right, Uncle Cole, but it's really exciting. Come on everybody, let's hit the slides," Summer trumpeted. She and Meadow started to run.

"Wait!" I called out. They skidded to a stop. "Back here, right now and put on some sunscreen."

I opened the container and squeezed out a handful of goopy liquid. I rubbed it all over Brooke. Meadow and Summer slathered it on each other. I made sure they covered every spot.

"How about Uncle Cole?" Summer asked.

I held the tube out for him.

"Nope. Don't need nothing like that."

"You'll burn without it."

"Me? No way. I've got a hide as tough as leather."

I tucked the sunscreen into my beach bag. "Meadow, Summer, you two stick together, okay?" They nodded impatiently. "I'll keep Brooke with me. Be careful, and if there are any problems you can find me in the little kids wading area."

"Yes, Mother," Summer chided me.

"And don't talk to any strangers, and if anybody bothers you then you speak to a lifeguard."

"Or yell for me," Cole interrupted. "And they won't bother you again." He was probably right about that. "What do you want me to do, Boss?"

"I don't know. I guess whatever you want. See you later." I took Brooke's hand and we toddled off to the kiddies' area.

* * * *

I'd watched Brooke slide down the little yellow slide about twenty-seven million times. Up the tiny steps, then down, shrieking in delight while holding my hand, splashing into the knee-deep water at the bottom. And up again. And again, and again and again.

All the other toddlers had a mother or father or both cooing over them, waving to them or using a video camera to record every precious moment. I felt sad for Brooke. All she had was me. And I had even less than that.

"I want some candy," Brooke said.

"No candy until after lunch, Brooky."

"I want lunch, then candy."

I looked at my watch. It was 11:30, a little early for lunch but I was hungry as well. By the time I rounded up the other two it would probably be noon. I hadn't seen them in over an hour. That would have worried me except Cole came over three or four times and he'd been talking to them. I guess he was so bored being here that he wandered over to see them because there was nothing better to do.

I picked up Brooke and walked toward the big water slides. There were five of them snaking down the side of the hill, emptying into a pool at the bottom. Each time one of the sliders hit the pool there was a scream of delight along with the splash. I took a seat on a bench overlooking the pool. There was nothing to do but wait for them to come down.

Off to the side, watching the sliders as well, was Cole. He was still wearing his jeans but he was now barefoot. It was the first time I'd seen him without his boots. They were always so shiny and he was continually rubbing the toe of one foot against the back of his other leg to keep them that way.

Even without them he still stood head and shoulders above everyone. The white of his body made his long black hair appear even darker, while the hair made his skin seem even whiter. The red bandanna and the bright colors of the dozen or so tattoos stood out brightly. He was sort of skinny and didn't have an ounce of fat on him. He lifted a hand and put it to his mouth. From his direction came a loud, piercing whistle. Then he waved.

I saw Meadow in the pool. She waved back at Cole as she waded away from the bottom of the slide and across the pool. I'd missed her coming down. At that instant Summer came into view and skidded across the surface of the pool before splashing under the water. Cole yelled out to her. She brushed the water away from her face, smiled and waved.

I watched in fascination as she and Meadow stood beside Cole. They were talking and smiling. He reached over and ruffled Meadow's hair. They were starting to run to the stairs back up to the top of the slides when I called out to them. They scanned the crowd, trying to find me. Brooke and I ran to them and they blurted out everything they'd done during the morning. We headed off together to get some food.

* * * *

We sat on the side of a grassy hill under the shade of a tree, polishing off burgers and fries. Brooke was continually negotiating how many bites of food she had to eat before she could get some candy.

"You have some nice tattoos," Summer commented.

"Yep, some of 'em are real special. This here one is my favorite." Cole pointed to a tiger dominating his upper left arm. It was black and red and orange and its eyes followed you eerily when you moved. I'd noticed it before as well.

"I like that one," Meadow said, pointing her finger at his other arm. "The snake."

"It's not just a snake, it's a cobra! Watch what happens when I do this!"

He flexed his arm and the tattoo seemed to move and undulate like a real snake.

"Cool!" Summer said with awe. "Which one do you like, Sky?"

"I don't know. Some of them are okay, but a couple are kind of crummy. They weren't all done by the same guy, were they?"

"Nope. Different people, different cities and even different countries."

"What countries?"

"This one was done in Mexico." He indicated a strange-looking Aztec figure. Underneath was a word I couldn't understand.

"What does that mean?"

"It's Spanish for warrior."

"You can speak Spanish?" I asked in astonishment.

"Nah. I'm still havin' trouble with English."

"Then why did you get him to put it in Spanish?"

"I don't know nothin' about it. Don't remember

a thing. I woke up, splitting headache, big gash on the side of my face, and found it there on my chest when I went to the can."

"How could you not remember getting a tattoo?"

"Last thing I remember was sitting in a bar and draining the last ounces out of a bottle of tequila."

"Does it hurt to get a tattoo?" Summer asked.

"Not that one . . . at least not that I can remember," Cole laughed. "Wanna find out?"

"What do you mean?" I asked.

"I figured after we're through here we could all go out and get tattoos," Cole replied.

"What?" I asked in disbelief.

"We could all get little matching ones . . . you know, to show we're a family."

"We can't do that!" I protested. "We can't get tattoos —"

"Sky!" Summer tried to interrupt.

"Joanne would get mad and it just isn't —"

"Sky! Uncle Cole's just joking."

I stopped. "Joking?"

"'Course I am. Lighten up a little won't ya, Sky."

I didn't like him putting one over on me. Meadow, Summer and even Brooke were chuckling away with him. Why weren't they on my side?

"What's that one?" Summer asked.

We all looked at a blackened patch on his upper right arm.

"Nothing. Just a tattoo I didn't want no more. Had it covered over."

"What was it?"

"I just said. Something I didn't want no more, so I don't want to talk about it."

"But I was just . . . "

"Drop it!" He rose from the grass and walked away. He took what was left of his lunch and tossed it into a garbage can.

"But what did I say?" Summer looked at me with tears in her eyes.

"Who knows? Don't worry about him. Forget it. Everybody get on some more sunscreen and then go back out and have some more fun."

I already had three kids to worry about. I couldn't waste any more time taking care of a fourth. I slopped some more sunscreen on Brooky, doing my best to stay calm on the outside. I prayed he wasn't going to leave . . . not just for now but for a long time.

Meadow and Summer listened while I gave them another safety lecture before they went to the wave pool. Brooky took me by the hand and dragged me back to the little yellow slide. On the way I noticed a group of girls about my age. There were five of them and they were giggling and laughing and talking. I felt an ache inside.

It had been so long since I'd had a friend. We were always moving. It was different for Summer and Meadow. Summer could make friends with a fence post and Meadow didn't seem to need friends, although she usually found a couple. I guess it had been easier for me too when I was younger. Little kids didn't seem to care where you lived or if your parents drove a fancy car or if you had the right kind of clothes . . . I never had the right clothes. Besides, I always had to take care of the girls and never had time to hang around with kids.

"Come on, Sky . . . come on," Brooke said, pulling on my arm.

I watched the girls fade into the crowd and then I picked up Brooke and waded into the water. It was cold but cold felt good. Brooke scrambled down and splashed up to the slide.

"You can't go in there!" a voice rang out a while later.

I turned and saw one of the lifeguards waving her arms at Cole. He was standing ankle deep in the wading pool. Brooke saw him as well and abandoned the slide to splash over to his side. I followed and arrived at the same time as the lifeguard.

"I'm sorry, sir, you can't go into the water without a bathing suit."

"I ain't got a suit. What's wrong with my jeans? So what if they get a little wet? No big deal."

"No sir, we're not worried about your jeans, but about what they can do to our filter system. We can't have the fibers go into our filters."

"What if I rolled them up so they wouldn't get wet?" Cole asked.

"Well . . . I guess that would be okay."

Cole muttered something under his breath but bent down anyway and started to roll up his pants. His legs were as white as his chest, although his shoulders and back did seem to have a reddish glow to them now. I was relieved there were no tattoos below his knees.

"Thought I could take over for a while . . . you know, give you a break," Cole said.

"I'm okay. I don't need a break."

"Sure you do. You're allowed to have a little fun too, you know. Go and have a few slides."

I thought about his offer. It would be nice to have a moment to myself, but what about Brooke? I was sure she wouldn't let me go without her.

"I'd like to, but —"

"But what?"

"I'm just worried Brooke will be too upset to let me go."

"She'll be fine with me. Come on, Brooke, give me your hand and I'll help you down the slide."

She let go of my hand and went with him without hesitation. I was glad but it bothered me how easily she went to him. He stood beside the little slide. He was taller than it. Brooke slid down and plopped into the water at the bottom. He helped her to her feet and she immediately headed back for the slide stairs. I watched this process repeat itself a dozen times.

Cole turned to me. "Sky, go. Have some fun. Slide a little . . . play with your sisters . . . do whatever."

"But —"

"Go! I'll take care of Brooke. She and I will have us some fun."

Still I hesitated.

"Don't worry. I'll watch out for strangers and we'll call you if somebody bothers us, okay?"

I couldn't help but smile. I went off to find Meadow and Summer. Maybe I could take a few turns down the slides, and watch them at the same time.

* * * *

A couple of times I snuck up on the wading pool to make sure he really was taking good care of her. They were never more than a few feet from the slide. Brooke was smiling and happy. Once I could hear them laughing before I could even see them. For whatever reason he seemed to like being around Brooke.

The thought popped into my mind that maybe he really was starting to care for us. It was a stupid thought and I pushed it out of my mind. This was about money, nothing else. A business arrangement.

I noticed how his shoulders were glowing a bright red. He'd got himself a good burn. His skin wasn't as tough as he thought it was.

Chapter 8

"You don't look like no lawyer to me!" Cole exclaimed.

"Well, man, you don't look like no parent to me, neither . . . but what say we try to work together anyway," Mr. Bailey answered.

A chuckle escaped from my lips.

"I'm glad you find this so amusing." Mr. Bailey and Cole gave me identical looks of annoyance.

"Why didn't you tell me about him?" Cole aimed a thumb at my lawyer.

"And more important, why didn't you tell me about him?" Mr. Bailey asked, pointing back at Cole.

Mr. Bailey spoke with a soft accent, a little like the Queen of England's husband or something. He was from Jamaica and he wore his hair twisted into shoulder-length dreadlocks that had small, colorful beads strung in them. I'd never seen him without a suit and tie.

"When you were asking me all those questions about your uncle, why didn't you tell me what he looks like. Why didn't you say something, Sky?"

"I don't know . . . I didn't think it mattered," I lied. I didn't tell him because I was sure that if I had he would have figured we didn't have a chance.

"You expect me to go into court presenting a guardian who looks like this?" He was asking a question as much as stating his opinion. "I'd get laughed out of court!"

"I expect that happens to you a lot," Cole said, chuckling.

"What do you mean?" Mr. Bailey demanded.

"You gotta expect people to laugh at you if you go into court looking like you just took your hair outta curlers and stuck bits of pretty plastic in it."

"Don't you go making fun of my hair . . . at least it gets washed now and again."

"I'm not here to take no garbage from nobody!" Cole thundered. "I'm outta here!" He jumped to his feet.

"Good!" Mr. Bailey replied, equally loud, rising to his feet as well.

"Wait! Just wait!" I yelled. I grabbed Cole by the hand and held onto him.

"Please, both of you, please. Could we just sit down? Please," I pleaded.

Cole had one hand on the doorknob. He stopped and turned around. He looked at me and then at Mr. Bailey.

"She's right, man. Please, come back and take a seat."

Cole nodded and came over to the desk. Mr. Bailey offered his hand and Cole shook it.

"Mr. Gray, my name is Bailey. I'm the children's lawyer and it is my job to represent their views in court. Sky, as well as Summer and Meadow, have told me they want to be with you. We have to present a plan to the court to support their wishes."

"Now we're talking. Call me Cole."

"Cole. Very good, Cole. Why don't you go calling me by my first name, Cephus."

"Sea fish. Your name is sea fish?"

"No, you don't say it like that. It's Cephus."

"What sorta name is that?"

"It's mine. And my father's, and his father's before him. Anything more you want to say about my name?"

"Nope. Just wondering. Seems like nobody involved in this thing has a near-normal name, that's all."

"Maybe you're right there, but the judge won't be interested in what anybody's called, and if we can present a good case, what you look like won't matter much either."

"What will matter?" Cole asked.

"Things like where you reside, what you do for

120

a living, who will take care of the children while you're at work, references, people who'll attest to what a wonderful person you really are, and —" he stopped, and a concerned look crossed his face. "We're in trouble, aren't we?"

I nodded. There was no doubt, we were in trouble.

* * * *

"I guess that just about ends it," Mr. Bailey said.

Cole and I got up and said our goodbyes. We were just starting out the door when Mr. Bailey called out to me.

"Could you stay for a moment, Sky, so we could talk . . . in private."

Cole nodded and left the room. He closed the door behind him.

"Sit, Sky." He gestured to a chair right beside him. I took the seat.

"I'm not too happy about any of this. I don't have a good feeling at all."

"He's our uncle and we want to live with him and nothing else matters."

"Much more matters, especially to a judge. For goodness sakes, Sky, he's a criminal, he has no house for you to live in, he's only been employed by that motorcycle shop for a short while, he doesn't have any money to support you and your sisters and lastly, he can't bring anybody into court as a reference. All those things matter."

"He isn't a criminal!" I protested. "He hasn't broken any laws for a long time. And me and Summer can speak for him."

"Even if that was enough, where will he find the money to support you? Where will you all live?"

"He has a job, and someday there'll be the insurance money," I said quietly. "You said before we could get some of it to help us."

"Some, but who knows how much there'll even be." He looked at me very seriously. "You can't count on that money and neither should your uncle."

"I understand. I better get going now. I don't want to keep him waiting." I headed for the door but stopped. I turned back to Mr. Bailey. "Do we have a chance?"

"Not a big one."

"I thought you were a good lawyer."

"I am, but I'm not a magician. I'll do my best."

"I guess that's all I can hope for."

He slowly closed his folder. "I'll try, Sky . . . I'll try."

* * * *

Meadow and Summer and I sat up front in the courtroom, behind a long table, with Mr. Bailey beside us. Joanne and the child-welfare lawyer sat at a table next to ours. The whole morning Mr. Bailey had argued that we should live with our uncle, on a trial basis. The agency lawyer tried to convince the judge they didn't want us to go any-where. He argued they were still looking for our fathers, who would have the legal right to claim us over our uncle, and wanted us to stay in care. As well, their lawyer pointed out that Cole didn't have a plan that would be suitable, even on an interim basis.

The judge listened and asked some questions and then adjourned the court until after lunch. I don't know how anybody could eat lunch. I was too nervous to do anything except pick at my food.

Back in court, my eyes were drawn to where Cole sat behind us. He looked so different. His earring was no place to be seen, his hair was neatly combed and tied back in a ponytail and his leather jacket and jeans had been replaced by a white shirt and dress pants. The pants were short and showed too much of his boots. I didn't know whether he didn't have any shoes or he was just so attached to those boots that he couldn't bear to wear anything else. They were so bright and shiny that they had a mirror quality. Every time I looked back, he was rubbing one boot or the other against the pant of the opposite leg. It was sort of like his version of me twirling my hair.

Mr. Bailey had met with Cole, Summer, Meadow and me on three occasions to get ready for court. In each meeting he'd stressed to Cole how he needed to change his appearance, and in every session Cole told him the only way he was going to change the way he looked was if Mr. Bailey would change the way he looked. Cole said they could go to the barber together and both get buzz cuts. That made it even more surprising when he did arrive all dressed up.

"All rise, court is back in session," the clerk called out.

We all rose to a chorus of scraping chairs. The judge swept into the room and took his place behind the bench.

"Please be seated," he called out and we all sat down.

The rustling quickly faded away and was replaced by dead silence, broken only by the sounds of papers being shuffled by the judge. He was looking down at his bench, acting as if we weren't even there. Finally he raised his head. He looked directly at me. I tried to read his expression, hoping for a hint, but found none.

"I have had an opportunity to explore the options that have been put before me today. I must admit there are very few times when I have seen two positions so opposed. There appears to be no room for compromise." He paused and took a sip from a glass perched on the corner of the bench.

"The agency has made a very thorough presentation of the reasons why they believe the children would best be served by remaining in care. In addition they have put forward concerns and questions regarding the ability and suitability of Mr. Gray to act as a guardian. Points which, I must admit, have a great deal of validity." He stopped and took another drink from his glass.

I could feel my heart sink. There was no chance. "What about us?" I asked nobody and everybody.

Mr. Bailey put a hand on my arm to quiet me down, but I pulled it away. "How can he make a decision without hearing what I have to say?"

"Sky, please —" Mr. Bailey began to say.

"Your lawyer is here to speak for you," the judge interrupted. "Hasn't he put your position forward?"

"What?"

"Has he told me where you want to be?" the judge asked.

"Yeah, but don't I get a chance to talk?"

"That would be acceptable. Please."

I stood up the way I'd seen everybody else stand when they were talking to the judge. "Look, I don't see why this is so hard. He's our uncle and he wants us and we want to be with him."

"I understand that, but there are many considerations involved," the judge replied.

"I don't know what you mean. All I know is that some guy — some drunk — killed our mother . . . took her away." Up until now every time I even thought about Mom I had to fight back the tears. And now when I needed a few tears, none came. I bit down hard on the inside of my cheek and winced in pain. "And now, now that we find our uncle . . . they want to take him away from us . . ." My voice cracked and I squeezed out a couple of tears. "We don't have anything . . . we just want to be with our family." I covered my eyes with my hands and sat back down. I made some noises that I hoped would sound like sobbing. If this performance didn't fool him than nothing would.

Mr. Bailey placed an arm around my shoulder. "Here take this," he said as he poured me a glass of water.

The judge cleared his throat. "Let me continue. On the other hand the legislation states I should pursue the least restrictive alternative. And of course we must consider the wishes of the children to be placed in the care of their uncle. I think Sky has expressed this very eloquently and emotionally. I know this decision will not be particularly popular with everybody."

We'd lost, despite everything.

"So I have decided to allow the children to be temporarily placed in the care of their uncle."

"What did he say?" I asked in shock.

The judge removed his glasses and peered down from the bench directly at me. "I said, young lady, we're giving you a chance at living with your uncle on a trial basis for the next three months."

I almost jumped out of my seat as Summer shrieked with delight. At almost the same instant I heard Cole yahoo from behind me.

"Your Honor, we strenuously object!" the agency's lawyer said as she rose to her feet.

"I think you made that clear during your submissions, did you not?" the Judge retorted.

"Well . . . yes, your Honor."

"Good. Now sit down and listen to my reasons." She meekly followed his directions.

"As I stated I, too, have significant reservations concerning the ability of Mr. Gray to provide for these children. However, these reservations are countered by the desire of both Mr. Gray and the children to be together and by the beginnings of a plan that has been proposed. In addition I am very disturbed by the agency's inability to provide even short-term stability for the children."

"I object to that remark!" the lawyer stated, jumping to her feet.

"That's good to know, since it truly is objectionable. These four girls were placed in one home on an emergency basis, then separated, and now the oldest is in her third setting. I do not wish to hear any arguments to support such a record, so be seated again."

For a second time the lawyer took her seat beside Joanne.

"During this interim placement the children will reside with their uncle and the child-welfare agency shall provide close and continuous supervision. If issues of concern arise, the agency is free to bring the matter back before the courts immediately. Are there any more questions?"

"None, your Honor," Mr. Bailey said, rising from his seat. "We are most grateful for your decision."

"Good. Now Mr. Gray, I wish to address myself specifically to you. I am doing the caring thing here today — not necessarily the smart thing but the caring thing. You will have the opportunity to provide for your nieces."

"Thanks," Cole answered.

"Don't thank me yet. All I've given you is a chance to demonstrate your suitability as a parent, or your lack of suitability."

"You can trust me, don't worry."

"Trust has nothing to do with it. What you need to be totally aware of is that if you do not prove yourself a suitable parental figure then you will have absolutely no chance of obtaining full guardianship. Do I make myself clear?"

"Yeah. Crystal."

"Is two weeks sufficient time for you to secure the house and prepare for the arrival of the girls?"

"Sure, two weeks should be enough time."

"Then my order will be in effect for two weeks from tomorrow. I order the agency to make all necessary arrangements for the children to be brought to their uncle's home — their new home — by noon on August the twenty-second. Court is adjourned."

Summer threw her arms around me and Meadow moved in close enough for me to capture her with one of my arms. I looked over their heads and saw Joanne looking at us. I'd expected her to be mad about losing the case, but instead she looked worried. I knew what she was thinking because my head and heart were both calling out the same message: what had I gotten us into?

Chapter 9

"Is that all your stuff?" Ed asked.

"Two bags," I answered. "Isn't that enough?"

"Enough for me. More bags just means more to carry."

Ed slammed the trunk shut and we climbed into the car. He started it up and we drove off.

"We have a lot more stuff. Furniture and dishes and things. They were put in storage when my mother . . ." I paused and swallowed hard. "When we had to come into foster care."

"And will the stuff stay in storage or will it be coming to the house?"

"To the house. Cole didn't have those sorts of things so I guess it's going to be all right. I wonder what our new place is like."

"It's nice," Ed answered.

"You've seen it?"

"Helped arrange for Cole to rent it. It belongs to a friend of a friend."

"What's it like?"

"Not big. You and Summer will have to share one room and Meadow and Brooke another."

"That's okay. We've never had our own rooms. Last place we lived the girls slept in the one bedroom and Mom and me shared a fold-out couch in the living room."

"That would be hard. This place also has a good location. Only a short walk across a park from the school Meadow and Summer will attend. It has a day-care center, and a spot has been reserved for Brooke. Your school is about half a mile away — easy walking distance."

"Sounds okay," I said.

"I guess that part is."

I knew without asking what he was getting at. You'd have to be a fool not to have doubts about Cole, and Ed was no fool.

"I'm there to help, to do things," I said.

"I know. And I know people are counting on you. As far as I'm concerned, counting on you too much."

"I don't understand."

"You're a smart kid, maybe too smart for your own good sometimes, but you're still a kid."

"I'm almost fifteen."

"That's what I said, just a kid. Kids need adults

to take care of them, not the other way around. Here, take this." Ed handed me a piece of paper.

"What is it?" I asked, unfolding it.

"My home telephone number. You need help, you call, and I'll come."

"We'll be fine," I protested.

"Maybe you will, but keep the number handy, just in case. Okay?"

"I guess."

"Don't guess, just call if I can help. Things will go wrong, and I know you won't be turning to Joanne. You'll be trying to hide anything bad from her."

"So why would I call you? You work for them too."

"No, I don't. I'm a volunteer. I don't work for nobody. I'm just a retired old geezer who does what he wants to do. And what I want to do is help you and your sisters. Understand?"

I nodded. I almost believed him.

"Good, and not a second too early. We're here."

Ed turned up the driveway of a bungalow that sat well back from the road, partially hidden behind bushes and shrubs and surrounded by a white picket fence. Already in the driveway was the old heap Cole now owned.

"This is it?"

"No, I drove to the wrong house by accident. What do you think?"

As Ed went to the trunk, I scanned the neighborhood. On either side were similar houses, all with big well-maintained lawns and beds filled with flowers. They looked like houses from some TV show or movie. I almost expected Mrs. Cleaver from *Leave It To Beaver* to come running out of the front door wearing an apron and carrying a plate of homemade cookies to welcome us to the neighborhood. Of course, if she saw Cole she'd take a second look, go home, lock her door and not let her kids out to play unsupervised.

Over the years, we'd lived in a lot of places — apartments, above stores and in big run-down buildings, old houses on the wrong side of town, or rickety shacks in the country — but none like this.

"Quiet is right." I wondered how the neighbors would feel when they found out who had snuck into their little world?

"It's a good place to raise kids."

"How would you know?" I asked.

"'Cause this is where I raised mine."

"I didn't know you had kids!"

"They're hardly kids now, but I have three of them. All grown up and on their own." Ed knocked on the front door. "This is the only time you'll have to knock on this door."

There was no answer. He turned the knob and the door swung open. The living room was piled high with boxes, and furniture was scattered around in no semblance of order. I recognized the furniture. It was Mom's — I guess ours now.

"Hello!" Ed called out. "We're here!" There was no answer.

"I guess he had to leave for a minute," I commented.

"He should have locked the door," Ed replied.

I wandered around the room. The boxes were piled haphazardly. I turned my head upside down to read the This Side Up labels, which were almost exclusively the wrong way. I turned over one of the boxes. How was I ever going to sort through all this stuff and set up house? I was suddenly hit with the reality of what I'd set in motion. Somehow I was supposed to care for my sisters and be their full-time parent, with nobody to help but Cole. I felt the blood drain from my body.

"Sky, are you okay?"

"Yeah, fine . . . why?"

"You're all white, and you're trembling."

The shakes were spreading throughout my body.

"You come right here," Ed said, taking me by the hand and sitting me down on a chair. "Have you eaten today?"

"I didn't feel hungry this morning."

"You need to eat! You just sit there and I'll see if there's any food in the place." He disappeared through the kitchen door.

I couldn't just sit there. I leaned forward to the nearest box and ripped off the masking tape sealing it shut. I opened the flaps. It was packed with stuff, just like I knew all the other boxes would be.

Ed came back into the room. "It's like Old Mother Hubbard's in there. The cupboards are bare but there was some juice in the fridge." He handed me a plastic container of orange juice. "Drink it from the bottle."

I took a big, long drink. It felt good going down.

"There sure is a lot of stuff. Glad I only had to bring in the two bags," Ed said. He ran his fingers through his graying hair, and let a whistle escape from his lips as he surveyed the room. "Where do we start?"

I had no idea where to begin. It didn't seem possible that this . . . What did he mean 'we'? "You have a golf game."

"Looks like I'm going to miss my tee-off time."

"You don't have to help," I protested.

"I don't have to do anything I don't want to. What I want to do is help."

I felt so relieved, I had to fight to keep my emotions inside.

"So do you want me to stay?" Ed asked.

"I guess."

Ed took a box and ripped it open. He pulled a plate from its newspaper wrappings. "Looks like this box goes in the kitchen," he said as he picked it up and started to walk away.

"Ed?" I called out.

He stopped part way through the door and looked at me.

"Thanks."

* * * *

About a half-hour after we started, Summer came in, alone. Her driver didn't even wait to see if anybody was home. She no sooner got in the door than I put her to work, too. She would have spent the entire afternoon going over the contents of a single box, but I kept barking at her to keep moving every time she slowed down.

I heard the front door open. I had been quietly stewing, wondering why Cole wasn't here to help with all the unpacking.

"It's about time!" I hollered from the kitchen. I stomped through the door to the living room, ready to give him a piece of my mind but stopped short. Joanne was standing there.

"Actually I'm early."

"Yeah, I guess you are." She was by herself. Where were the girls? I was struck by a sudden fear they weren't coming. "Where are Brooke and Meadow?"

"I still have to get them. I was at an appointment near here and called Debbie. Brooke had just gone to sleep. I thought I could help out around here for a while."

The rock in my stomach melted away. "Help out or snoop around?"

Joanne smiled. "I guess a little of both. Where's your uncle?"

"He had to go out for a while."

"When will he be back?"

"Soon, he had to go to work." That sounded like a good excuse, one nobody could get too upset about.

Ed called out. "The beds are all set up." He came into the living room and saw Joanne. "Great, another pair of hands. Where do you want her to work, Sky?"

"I want to set up the kitchen a certain way. Her help wouldn't help. Where's Summer, maybe Joanne can work with her?"

"She's in her bedroom, or should I say, your bedroom. She unpacked a box of stuffed animals she keeps arranging and rearranging on her bed."

"And you're letting her?" I demanded as I started to walk down the hall. Ed grabbed me by the arm and stopped me.

"Let her unpack like a kid. It's bad enough you can't be young too. Leave her alone."

I nodded slowly and he let go of my arm.

"Joanne can start by opening up all the boxes and taking them to the right rooms to be unpacked. I'll keep on working in the kitchen," I said.

* * * *

"I don't know where this one goes," Ed said as he came into the kitchen with a box.

"Just put it down here and I'll have a look," I answered from the top of the stepladder.

He put the box down on the table and left.

I looked at the carton. There wasn't anything written on it. Inside were neatly folded clothes. I pulled out a sweater, but before it even cleared the box I knew it didn't belong to any of us . . . it was Mom's.

It made sense her clothes would have been packed too. But it was still a shock. Gently, I cradled the sweater. I ran my fingers along the soft material. It was typical of everything she wore: soft, fuzzy pastel sweaters and long, flowing flowery skirts and dresses. I pressed my nose into the knitted folds and inhaled the faint fragrance of the perfume she always used. The scent brought it all back . . . not just who my mother was, but all that was gone, and how all I had left of her were a few pieces of clothing and the faint lingering smell of her perfume. The sob started deep in my chest. I held the sweater tight against my face to muffle the sound. I didn't want anybody to hear me cry — crying was weak and I needed to be strong for everybody.

Later I stashed the box, along with two others, in the basement crawl space. I couldn't bear to go through them right now. But I kept the sweater and put it under my pillow.

Joanne entered the room and took a seat at the table. "Sky, we need to talk about Brooke."

I put down the pots I was stacking in the cupboard and straightened up. "What about her? Is something wrong?" I asked anxiously.

"Come and sit down." Joanne patted a chair.

"I don't want to sit down! Is something wrong?"

"No, no, she's all right. It's just —"

"Just what?" I demanded.

"You're going to have to be a little patient with her when she arrives. She's having a hard time with all of this," Joanne said.

"I know. It's hard to live with strangers."

"That's not what I mean. The hard time isn't about being in care. It's about having to leave."

"What are you talking about?"

"She's pretty attached to Debbie and Jack, and she's had a rough time since we told her she was going to be leaving."

"She's coming back to us! Back to her family."

"I know you're her family —"

"I don't want to hear any more of this!"

Just then I heard the unmistakable sound of the Harley pulling up to the house. I pushed by Joanne and ran out the front door. Cole climbed off his bike and popped it up on the kickstand. I raced over and threw my arms around his neck because I knew Joanne was watching.

"Joanne is inside. I told her you had to go to work," I whispered in his ear.

"I was at work."

"Can't you say it a little more believably?"

"I was at work."

"That's better, but you don't have to convince me as long as Joanne believes it."

"Kid, you don't understand. I was at —" He paused. "Aw, forget it. Let's go inside and unpack."

Chapter 10

"I ain't got time for this. I gotta get to work!" Cole hit his hand against the table, and the dishes rattled.

"It won't take too long, just a few minutes," I replied. Why did he always have to act like such a baby?

"Why can't you do it? I thought you were goin' to take care of all the parenting stuff."

"I tried. The school secretary said a parent or guardian had to be there to register them. She wouldn't let me. It's a rule."

"A stupid rule. Typical. How 'bout I write you a letter and —"

"I already did that when I registered at my school."

"What do you mean?"

"I wrote a letter and forged your signature at the bottom." Not only did this save me the embarrassment of him showing up at my school, but it let me know that if I could sign his name once it might come in handy another time.

"You forged my signature?" he said, shaking his head.

"Yeah, it wasn't hard. Your writing looks like chicken scratches."

"Then do the same thing for the girls' school," he suggested.

"I tried. The secretary said it wasn't good enough, so you'll have to come and do it. There's no choice."

"Fine," he answered, getting up from the table.

I almost did a double take. That was exactly what Mom always said when she meant the exact opposite of fine. This wasn't the first time I'd heard her words or way of saying things come out of his mouth. Mom and Cole didn't look a lot alike except for around the eyes, but there was something of her inside him and I didn't know whether that made me feel good or unnerved me.

"Earth to Sky! Snap out of it and let's get moving!"

"Oh, okay, fine," I answered, imitating the way he'd said it.

Cole changed into his work clothes while I got Brooky dressed and directed Summer and Meadow to clear away the kitchen dishes. We moved so quickly that he was still getting ready as we stood at the front door.

"Do you want us to wait in the car?" Summer asked.

"Naw. You all better walk over. I want to head to work right after I finish up this school stuff."

"Couldn't you take the car to work?"

"That heap? I'd be the laughing stock of the whole garage. People who work on Harleys don't drive cars! I don't even like 'em to know I own one. Besides, I can make a lot better time on my bike."

"Okay, we'll meet you over there. Come on everybody," I called out as Brooky snuggled into my chest. It felt good. With each day she was more like herself again. Thank goodness we got her back when we did. Things had been difficult with Brooky for the first few days. She had trouble getting to sleep at night and broke into tears easily. I hated to admit it but Joanne had been right. There was more to Joanne than I originally thought.

We crossed the street and walked along a path to the schoolyard. The soccer field and baseball diamond were completely deserted. A bunch of teenagers were slumped under a tree at the far side of the field. Although we'd only been here a week, I'd seen them a few times before. They were hard to miss. They were always talking and laughing too loud and generally acting like idiots.

A couple lived on our street. I'd seen one of them when I registered myself at my new school the day before and we'd exchanged a few words. I'd wanted to say more, but I just didn't know what to say. Besides, what was the point? I had too much to do.

We circled around to the front of the school. It had a big curving driveway and a nearly deserted parking lot off to the side. A group of women stood just outside the doors. Little kids buzzed around them as they talked. I took a seat on a bench under a sign that read Sawmill Valley Public School, and my sisters crowded in beside me. There was no sign of Cole.

In our rush to get out of the house, I hadn't wiped off Brooke's face. She had juice stains around her mouth and crusted, dried oatmeal on one cheek. Meadow wasn't much better. Her face was clean but her clothes were dirty.

One of the women looked us over and gave us a little smile, a smile that said she was better than we were and she didn't think we belonged here. It was hard to argue the last part. I felt so out of place in this neighborhood. I turned away.

The women continued their discussion and I listened in. They were talking about dance classes and piano lessons, and which teachers weren't good enough to teach their children and where there was a sale on carpeting. It all sounded foreign to me. They jumped from topic to topic and I was struck by the fact that everybody was talking, but nobody really seemed to be listening.

Just as I was getting really annoyed because Cole had rushed us to get ready only to keep us waiting, I heard his bike. One thing about riding a Harley, he'd never sneak up on you. It was a loud, raspy sound that rumbled up from the ground and settled into the pit of your stomach.

I'd asked Cole about how he could stand it so loud. He told me it was just like the purring of a kitten or the cooing of a baby. It was music to his ears. He said it was good to be loud because it meant people in cars noticed. Louder was safer because there were so many jerks on the road who didn't bother looking over their shoulder when they changed lanes, and this way they'd at least hear the bike before they knocked it down. Cole said there are only two kinds of bikers — those who've been knocked down by cars and those who haven't . . . yet.

Cole rolled up the driveway and then right onto the walk around the drive. Cole almost always parked on sidewalks. The engine died, he climbed off and popped the bike onto its stand.

The women had stopped talking. They were just standing there staring at Cole. Their children clung to their mothers' sides.

Cole folded his gloves into his helmet and tucked it under his arm. As he came toward us the woman all turned away in unison.

"I hope he's not here to register his children," one whispered.

"Don't be silly. There's nobody like him living around here," answered another. She had a gigantic diamond ring on one finger.

"Maybe he's a new teacher," yet another suggested and they all dissolved into a fit of nervous giggles. Boy were they funny.

I leaned over and whispered into Summer's ear. "Did you give Uncle Cole a hug this morning?"

"Yeah . . . I think I did."

"A second one wouldn't hurt, would it?"

Summer got up from the bench and ran right past the gaggle of women. She threw her arms around Cole as they all stared in disbelief, their mouths open but suddenly silent. Then I felt a rush of anger at these women, and was shocked by my response. Why would I have expected their reaction to be any different? Being around him so much, I'd been getting a little bit desensitized to the way Cole looked. I'd tried to convince myself that looks could be deceiving, that you couldn't judge a book by its cover, that appearance is only skin deep. The biggest problem was that Cole was more like a comic book, and those covers usually don't lie.

The group of women stood in the middle of the narrow sidewalk, frozen in place.

"'Scuse us, ladies," Cole said.

Like they'd been given a blast from a blow torch, the women thawed, and jumped out of the way, landing on the driveway on one side and the grass on the other. As we all walked together into the school I could feel eyes burning into the back of my head.

I knew that, possibly before we'd even finished registering today, and definitely before we'd gone to sleep tonight, the word would spread. Maybe they wouldn't like having us in the neighborhood, but they sure would enjoy having us to talk about.

The halls, which stretched in two directions, were dark. The only light came from the office and it cast illumination into the foyer and the entrance to the library across the way. The clicking of Cole's boots against the hard floor echoed down the hallway. He turned into the office and we followed.

A counter divided the office. Behind it was a PA system, a water cooler and three desks, each with a computer and telephone. On our side a row of chairs hugged the wall where a few framed pictures of children's artwork hung. There were almost identical pictures in every school I'd ever been in — semi-stick people, balloons, rainbows and dogs, names printed crooked and at least one *s* backwards. Summer and Meadow sat down in two of the seats and I dumped Brooke into a third.

A man stood on the opposite side of the counter, talking to a woman on our side. They were immersed in conversation and didn't even look over at us. Cole cleared his throat. They continued to talk, still not looking in his direction. They chattered away about their summer vacations. Cole cleared his throat again, but the sound was lost beneath a burst of laughter from the woman in response to something the man said.

"Are you two goin' to be through gabbing soon?"

The man looked up at Cole and his mouth dropped open and his eyes grew wide. The woman mirrored the same shocked expression. She took a small step away from Cole.

"I ain't got no time to listen to anybody jabbering. Why don't you get to work so I can get to work," he boomed, pointing a finger at the man.

"I better get going," the woman responded as she clumsily gathered up some pictures off the counter.

"I'm here to fill out papers to register my girls."

"Girls?" the man asked.

"Yeah, girls. Meadow, Summer, come on over here."

Summer instantly got up and came to the counter. Meadow slowly and reluctantly followed after.

"Now where are those papers I gotta sign."

"I — I'm not sure . . . I don't do that sort of thing."

"Well then why don't you get me somebody who can do that sort of thing."

Cole leaned over the counter until he was practically over top of the man. It was what I'd seen him do with Joanne before and it had the same chilling effect. The man cowered and backed away.

"I'll get my secretary. Mrs. Russell?" he called out weakly, his voice cracking over the final syllable. "Mrs. Russell!" he called louder.

A woman poked her head out of an adjoining room. I could see her and she could see me but Cole was just out of her field of view, blocked by a pillar.

"I hope you brought a parent this time."

"Yes, she did. This ah . . . gentleman." He stumbled over the word gentleman.

"I'll be there in a moment. Have them take a seat." She disappeared into the room.

"No!" the man practically yelled.

She poked her head back out.

"I need you to register them right now. I have things to do . . . in my office." He turned toward us. "Welcome to Sawmill Valley. I hope you'll enjoy the school. Remember my door is always open for students and parents. Goodbye."

He rushed into a room off the main office and slammed the door. The sign read Principal.

"So much for his door always being open," Cole said quietly. I snickered.

The secretary visibly startled as she rounded the corner and caught sight of Cole. She recovered very quickly. "So you finally brought along your father," she said.

"He isn't my father. He's our guardian," I answered.

"And our uncle," Summer added.

"As long as he has the authority to sign the registration papers. Fill out all of the spaces on these sheets and then sign your name here," she indicated, pointing with her pen to the bottom of the paper. Then she turned and disappeared once again.

Cole's forehead crinkled up. "I don't know some of this stuff."

"You probably don't know any of this stuff. Here, let me fill it out and you just put your signature at the bottom."

I grabbed the forms from him. He looked annoyed but relieved. I always had to fill out forms for my mother because she was always forgetting things. I picked up the pen and quickly put down the information. I didn't have answers to a couple of the questions; we didn't have a family doctor for one thing. I made up a name and phone number to put in the space. I handed Cole the pen and pushed back the forms. He signed his name at the bottom of both forms. Mrs. Russell reappeared in time to see him do this.

"Finished?"

"Yep, here they are."

She ran a finger down one form, checking each line. Then she did the same with the second.

"Meadow and Summer. What unusual names."

"I guess it takes a little getting used to," Cole said. I knew it sure took him a while.

"But you know," he began again, "we didn't want them to have old-fashioned, boring names. Names like, I don't know . . . Doris or Jean or Carol."

The woman made a huffing sound. She gathered the papers and walked across the office, stopping by a table at the far end.

"Wonder if she's Doris, Jean or Carol?" Cole said, so quietly I could barely hear him.

I looked at him. Now what? He motioned with his hand. There was a nameplate on each of the three desks; Doris, Jean and Carol were the first names.

"Is that it?" Cole asked, impatient again.

"I don't know," I replied.

"Hey!" he called out. The secretary turned around. "I gotta get to work. You need me anymore or what?"

"I think that's all we require."

"Good, I'll see you tonight. I won't be home till late so you fix supper for everybody," he instructed.

"No fair!" Summer objected. "We like it when you cook . . . no offence," she said, turning to me.

I didn't say anything. Cole had made supper the last two nights and the kids all loved his cooking.

"Your sister's a good cook, Summer. I'll see you three before bedtime." He started to walk out, but

Summer wouldn't let him leave until she gave him another hug.

The secretary, who looked like a Doris to me, looked up at us.

"Wouldn't it have been easier if you'd just let me register my sisters?" I asked.

She didn't say a word, but she did smile in response.

Chapter 11

The ringing of the phone exploded in my head and I sat bolt upright in bed, my heart pounding like it was going to come through my chest. For an instant I couldn't figure out where I was and I panicked. The phone rang again, and in the stream of light coming under and around the partially closed bedroom door, I could see Summer sleeping peacefully, and it all came back. I took a deep breath to steady myself. The third time, the phone was interrupted mid-ring and I heard Cole's voice. The clock on my dresser glowed out the time: 12:26.

There was no point in trying to get back to sleep. Even without the phone ringing I was waking up in the middle of the night with my mind racing and heart pounding, unable to get back to sleep.

Though I couldn't make out the words, I could hear Cole talking on the phone. He always used what Mom used to call an outdoor voice.

Summer was breathing softly. The sleep of the innocent. There was a small smile on her face and she'd kicked off the covers. I climbed out of bed and tucked her in. I was totally awake. I opened the door and took a few tentative steps in the direction of Cole's voice. The light coming from the living room partially illuminated the hallway, more on one side than the other. I pressed myself against the darker side and moved forward until I could see into the living room.

Cautiously I poked my head around the corner. Cole was at the far end of the room, his back to me, the receiver against his ear.

"What do you think you're doing?"

My heart jumped for a split second before I realized he wasn't talking to me but to the person on the other end of the line.

"Have you bought anything yet?"

What did he mean 'bought anything'? Was he talking about a drug deal? I'd heard about bikers being involved with drug dealing.

"Good. Don't be stupid. Don't do anything. Just stay there . . . Where are you? Murphy's Bar. Yeah, I know it. Isn't that the same place as last time?"

He was describing a drug deal, there couldn't be any other explanation.

"I want you to understand what I'm saying. You buy anything and you're as good as dead. Do you understand, good as dead. Just sit tight, I'm coming . . . yeah, of course, I know what time it is . . . just shut up . . . I'll be there. And remember, if you buy before I get there, your life is over! You're dead!" He slammed the phone down and I couldn't help but jump.

"Damn idiot! Damn fool!" he said loudly as I scurried back down the hall and into my room. My head was spinning. He wasn't just talking about a drug deal. He was going to kill somebody! The front door slammed and then there was the unmistakable sound of his heels clicking against the front walk. I stood in the semidarkness of my room and listened for the sound I knew would come next. Almost instantly the rumble of the Harley came in through the open bedroom window. I ran into the living room and peered through the window as the headlights moved down the driveway and disappeared. The rumble lingered on before fading to silence.

I walked to the door. He'd left us all alone in the middle of the night, without telling anybody or leaving a note, and he hadn't even bothered to lock the front door! I started to turn the lock and then realized if I locked the door he'd know somebody had been awake, and I didn't want him to know anything. Of course, I couldn't sleep with the door open, but then, who was I trying to fool?

I wouldn't be able to get back to sleep again anyway.

I snuggled down into the big easy chair. From here I could watch the front door and hear him coming so I could get back into bed without him noticing me. I'd spent more than one late night in this chair waiting for Mom to get home. More than enough.

I wondered what the neighbors would think about being woken up in the middle of the night by the sound of a motorcycle. I wondered when he'd be back. I wondered what he was going to do. Most important, I wondered what I'd got us into.

I thought about Joanne. Maybe she was right. Maybe everybody was right. I was being stupid and selfish. Maybe the girls would have been better staying where they were. Meadow liked Debbie and Jack, and Brooke was always talking about the things her foster mother did for her, like fixing her bubble baths, reading stories and cutting the crusts off her sandwiches. I was trying the best I could to be a good parent and to take care of everything and everybody. Why was it always up to me? Even before she died it always seemed to be up to me.

I could feel tears well up in my eyes.

"I am not going to cry!" I said aloud, and my words echoed off the walls. "He's not going to make me cry! Nobody is going to make me cry!"

I felt a surge of anger building in my chest and I knew I wouldn't. Tears were useless — they didn't do anything. At least anger gave you the power to go on.

Chapter 12

"Come on, Sky, go to the movies with us tonight," Julia said.

I swallowed a mouthful of my lunch. "I can't."

"It's a good movie. Don't you want to see it?" Christina asked.

"I do." I balled up my lunch bag and tossed it into the garbage can. All around us kids were talking and laughing and eating their lunches. I was so grateful to have a couple of friends to eat with — sitting there by myself the first few days made me feel like some sort of freak.

"How about if we go tomorrow night instead?" Julia asked.

"Or we can even wait until the weekend," Christina suggested.

"You're going to have to wait longer than that

if you want me to come along," I said.

"How long?"

"Well . . . in about two years Summer should be old enough to take care of Meadow and Brooke."

"I can't believe your uncle won't give you a night off," Julia stated.

I didn't answer. I guess maybe he would if I asked, but I didn't want him taking care of my sisters. There was only one person I trusted and that was me.

Julia made a face like she'd just bitten down on something sour, and my eyes followed her gaze. Coming across the cafeteria was a group of girls we all knew and hated. The most annoying were Rachel and Vanessa. They gave anybody they didn't think was as cool as them a hard time. That meant just about all of us because they were positive nobody was on their level of coolness, which was defined as occasionally skipping school or talking back to a teacher.

"Are you sure you can't come?" Christina asked.

"I guess I could," I said, "if we go now."

"Now! What do you mean?" Julia asked.

"We cut classes this afternoon and catch a matinee."

"We can't just skip school!" Christina protested.

"Yeah, my mother will kill me if she finds out I went to a movie instead of school."

"Then don't tell her," I suggested.

"I won't, but the school will," Julia explained, "if I don't bring a note."

"Oh, but you will bring one."

"I don't understand," Julia said.

I opened my notebook and turned to a blank page. In large, clear letters, I wrote a letter excusing Julia because she had a doctor's appointment.

"What's your mother's name?" I asked.

"Anita Daniels, but why do you want to know?" Julia asked.

"Because it'll look pretty stupid if I sign the letter, 'from Julia's mother.'"

"But you can't just forge a letter!"

"Of course I can, and it isn't even hard. See for yourself." I handed Julia the note.

"What I meant is that this can't work," Julia continued.

I smiled. "You remember when I was away last Friday afternoon?"

"Of course I do. Wait — are you saying you skipped school and forged a note to cover?" Christina asked.

My smile grew. I'd been feeling beat — going to school, doing my homework and taking care of my sisters, combined with the poor sleep I'd been having. I didn't really do anything special. I just stayed around the house, watched the soaps and even fell asleep for a while before I picked up the girls after school.

"But still —" Julia said.

"Why don't we give it a try," Christina interrupted.

"Are you kidding?" Julia said in shock.

"No, I think we could all use a break. Let's do it!"

* * * *

There weren't many people in the theater and the three of us sat right down by the front. It wasn't a bad movie, maybe not as good as I'd heard, but I didn't care. It just felt so good to be sitting here in the dark with Christina and Julia. I couldn't even remember spending time with friends — or at least people who were becoming my friends.

I'd had just enough to pay for my admission and buy a Coke and a small buttered popcorn. That left me with thirty-five cents of the twenty dollars I'd taken out of Cole's wallet. He left it on the top of the fridge one night, and I'd looked in it more out of curiosity. I wanted to see if there were any more pictures, but there were just scraps of paper, coins and crumpled-up bills. I took one — he probably wouldn't even notice. He could hardly keep track of anything, so there was no way he'd miss one bill.

Besides, it wasn't like I wasn't working hard enough to deserve some money or that he wasn't going to get a lot of our money when the lawsuit was settled. What did a few dollars matter? The only part that confused me was why I felt any guilt at all . . . but I did.

Chapter 13

Cole was out by the garage fiddling with his Harley. You'd figure, after spending all day at the motorcycle shop fixing bikes, the last thing he'd want to do when he got home was work on another one. Yet he was always polishing and cleaning and tinkering with it.

And not just his own either. Not long after we moved in he did some work on Ed's Indian and then on some of Ed's friends' bikes. They were all so pleased with his work that they told some of their friends, and now there always seemed to be somebody there with a bike. Ed had even helped Cole install a second telephone, a business line, in the house. I felt stupid saying "Cole's Chop House" when I answered it.

At least it was quieter with him outside, which

made it easier for me to do my homework. I'd missed a couple of assignments already and they were threatening me with a suspension if my work wasn't done. I just didn't understand some of the things I was studying. Bouncing around from school to school, I'd missed learning things that everybody else knew. It didn't help that some days I was so tired I had to fight to stay awake in class. Even worse I'd missed a surprise test in math when I cut classes to go to the movies.

Meadow was outside with Cole. She always ran out the door the instant she heard the sound of his bike coming down the street and greeted him before he even had a chance to get his helmet off. I really wasn't happy about her getting too close to him. You had to stay faithful to your family first and he was only family in name. Besides, there was no telling how long this whole thing would last. I didn't need to have problems with Meadow when he disappeared the way I had when Brooky left the foster home.

I'd pored over the newspapers for days after he'd charged out in the middle of the night, but I hadn't read anything about a killing. I'd almost convinced myself the whole thing had been a misunderstanding or just my imagination. Still, I didn't trust him, and I wouldn't allow myself to like him, no matter what he said or did.

Joanne had stopped by for a while before Cole got home. She was always dropping over.

Sometimes she made appointments and other times she just showed up. She really wasn't a bad person, especially when she stopped talking like a social worker. She was really pretty smart about some things, and last week she helped me with an English assignment that had me totally mystified. Today we talked about the kids and school, and I'd shocked myself by telling her how hard it was to have no real friends. She seemed to really understand what I meant. I didn't know her age exactly, but I figured she was closer to my age than I was to Brooky. She probably remembered being fifteen — well almost fifteen. She said she understood what it was like to be lonely because she was lonely herself. She was raised in a different city, far from here, where her family still lived. She told me how much she missed them.

It was funny but when we were sitting around the table that afternoon, I had a terrible urge to tell her about the phone call and ask her what she thought. But, of course, I didn't. Maybe she did care, or maybe this was just what social workers did to get you to trust them so you'd let down your guard.

"How long till supper?" Summer asked as she walked into the kitchen, trailed by Brooke. Summer was playing Barbies with Brooke to keep her amused and out of my hair while I studied.

"You're asking the wrong person," I answered.

"Is Uncle Cole going to cook again tonight?" Summer asked.

"Hasn't he made supper almost every night for the past seven weeks?" I asked in response.

Cole had been home to make dinner for us almost every night since we'd moved in. I was shocked the first time I found him puttering in the kitchen. He wouldn't even let us in the kitchen when he was "creating." He told us there was a genius at work and not to bug him.

"I'm hungry. Will supper be ready in a couple of whiles?" Brooke asked.

"Maybe even in one while," I answered. I closed my books, stacked them and took them off the table.

"Summer, you and Brooky set the table and I'll go find out about supper."

I glanced at my watch. It was getting late if Cole was going to follow his usual routine. Each week-night, after supper, he went out just before seven, leaving me to clean up the dishes and get the kids settled into bed. He was usually back by nine, although a few times he didn't return until closer to eleven. I tried not to think about what he was doing, although I knew for sure he wasn't going back to work because he didn't come home all covered with grease the way he did from the shop.

Cole was lying on his back on the pavement beneath the engine of his bike. Meadow was squatting down beside him. Tools and pieces of engine were scattered around them in a semicircle.

"What's wrong with the bike?" I asked.

"Carburetor," Meadow answered matter-of-factly.

"Carburetor?"

"Probably," Cole confirmed looking up at me. "I felt a little flutter when I was accelerating."

"What do you mean by a flutter?"

"The engine just didn't sound right . . . it seemed a bit rough."

"It always sounds rough!" I exclaimed.

"Maybe to your ear it's all just noise, but to me it's like music, and I know when something's not playing the right note."

"You really do like this sort of thing, don't you?" I asked.

"Fixing bikes? 'Course I do. There's something real special about figuring out what's wrong and trying to make it right. It's like a jigsaw. Do you like puzzles?"

"No, hate 'em," I answered. I had enough real-life problems to solve.

"Pass me a two-inch socket wrench," Cole said.

"What is a —" I started to say.

"Here," Meadow responded, handing him a tool.

"Thanks."

I gave Meadow a questioning look. She smirked knowingly.

"Do you want me to start supper?" I asked.

"No!" Meadow protested. "I want Uncle Cole to cook."

It was nice of him to cook, but I still felt a

twinge of hurt that everybody liked his meals better than mine.

"I'll be fixing it," Cole answered.

"Mexican?" Meadow asked.

"What else?"

"We're running short of time . . . if you're planning on going out," I cautioned.

"This is nearly fixed. Won't take much longer. And I am heading out tonight," he said quietly.

I hadn't asked him where he went each night and he never volunteered the information. He just said he was going out or had to meet some people. It was probably better I didn't know where he was going or who he was meeting.

I changed the subject. "How come everything you make is Mexican?"

"You complaining?"

"No! Not at all," I said hurriedly. It was always really good. "I just wanted to know, that's all. Where did you learn about Mexican food?"

"Down south. Lived in Texas, California and across the Rio Grande in Mexico as well. Burritos, tacos, enchiladas and refried beans is just the beginning of things. By the time I get through with the bunch of you, you'll be practically speaking Spanish."

I wondered if his record had been clean the last while because he'd been committing crimes in other countries and there was just no record of them. I remember reading some place about how drugs come over the border from down south.

"Sounds like you've lived in a whole lot of other places," I commented.

"All over North America and down to the tip of South America. When I left that foster home twenty years ago I tried to get as far away as I could from this city. Never wanted to see this place again."

"Then why did you come back?" I asked.

"It's hard to explain . . ." He paused and looked at Meadow. "Go on up to the house and get yourself all cleaned up."

She nodded and stood up. Her hands and shirt were covered with grease and grime.

What did he want to say that he didn't want Meadow to hear? "Wash up good, Meadow. I want the dirt down the drain and not on my towels, okay?" I asked.

She continued walking without even turning around or acknowledging my warning.

"Meadow!" Cole called out. She stopped and turned.

"Do what your sister said."

She smiled, nodded and was off again. Why didn't she listen to me like that anymore? A dozen times over the past few weeks the kids had looked to him for direction instead of me. Who did they think was really in charge here anyway?

"You asked why I came back," Cole said as he slid out from under the bike and sat beside it.

I nodded, my thoughts interrupted.

"When you're fixing an engine you gotta look at not just what's wrong but what made it go wrong. Understand?"

"Not a word," I admitted.

"It's like dominos. You knock one down and it knocks the next and that knocks the next one and it knocks the —"

"I get the idea, but what's that got to do with fixing bikes or why you came back here?"

"It's all the same. I needed to return to the beginning to figure out where it started to go wrong."

"Where what started to go wrong?" I asked.

"My life . . . my whole stinking life."

The entire time we'd been talking, Cole had been working, his eyes locked on his bike. Now he turned and looked directly at me.

"I came back to talk to my parents . . . my adoptive parents."

"And you found them?" I asked.

He nodded.

"What did they tell you?"

"Nothing."

"Nothing? They wouldn't even talk to you?"

"Dead people don't talk."

A terrible thought exploded in my mind. I knew how much he hated them and I wondered if he'd been responsible for their deaths.

"The old man's been dead for over ten years and my adoptive mother for almost five. She wasn't that bad, at least compared to him."

I felt a rush of relief even though I knew what I was thinking had been ridiculous.

"Wasted a lot of time hating people who were already dead." He paused and shook his head and stared off into the distance. "Funny, I wished them dead for years and then, when I found out they were gone, I felt ... I felt ... I don't know ... something else."

I was at a complete loss for words.

"Went out to the cemetery to see where they were buried."

I shuddered. I hated cemeteries.

"You believe in fate?" Cole asked.

"Not really. Mom believed in it completely and look where it got her."

"Well I believe in it. Were you told how the agency found me?"

"Through the adoption registry thing," I answered.

"Yep, but here's the fate part. When I was at the cemetery, standing by my parents' graves, I saw a funeral going on. Big hearse, cars, lots of people dressed in black, flowers. And I got to thinking about my parents' funerals — what it would have been like, who would have been there . . . and how I wasn't there because nobody would've known where to look. Heck, I can't even remember where I was when either of them died. Do you understand?"

"Yeah, but I don't know what any of this has to do with fate."

"Keep listening. I was thinking about how nobody knew where I was. Then I got thinking about my family, my real family, and wondered if my sister, or maybe even my mother, had been searching for me. And then I remembered about how I once put my name on that adoption list. So I drove out of the cemetery and went straight to a pay phone and looked up the number and called. I just knew, just knew, I was being led back to them, that all I had to do was call and they'd be listed right there. So this woman answers the phone, and after I explain everything she puts me on hold so she can check. And while I was waiting I even said a prayer, a long prayer. Right there in the phone booth I dropped to my knees and prayed, the phone still stuck to the side of my head. Bet you have trouble picturing me doing that?"

He was right. I didn't have that big an imagination.

"So finally the woman comes back and tells me there's no matching registration. Nobody wanted to get in touch with me. Nobody. I felt like somebody had kicked me in the stomach . . . or a foot lower. If I hadn't already been on my knees, I think I would have fallen over. I was just going to hang up when the lady asks if I'm still at the same address or did I want to update my file? I don't know why, I didn't have any hope left, but I gave her my new address. Two days later I heard from Joanne. Fate."

"Just dumb luck," I answered. "You can't get through life relying on luck. I was always telling my mother she had to plan for things, but she never listened. Never!" I snapped angrily.

"Your mamma's buried around here somewhere, isn't she?" Cole asked. He rose to his feet.

I nodded.

"I need to go out and pay my respects. You haven't been out to her grave since the funeral, have you?"

"No, of course not."

"Probably still too soon. We'll go out sometime . . . bring fresh flowers, help you girls to remember things about her."

"I remember enough!" I was shocked by the anger in my voice.

Cole reached over and placed a hand on my shoulder. "It wasn't her fault, Sky. Don't be angry. She didn't want to go and die."

"Of course she didn't want to die! How can you say I'm angry at her for dying!" I snapped. I tried to turn away, but he tightened his grip on my shoulder and held me firmly in place.

"You are angry at her. If it ain't for dying, it's gotta be for the way she lived. I know that sometimes she didn't do the right things for you kids."

"Shut up!" I yelled. "Shut up right now!" I screamed. "And let go of me!" A bolt of white hot anger surged up from the pit of my stomach and burned away the tears starting to form in my eyes.

"I'll let you go if you hear me out. Okay?" he asked.

I didn't answer, and glared at him instead.

"Okay?" he asked again.

I nodded and he released his grip.

"I've heard some of the things you girls have said about living with your mother. I know she didn't always do some things right. But I also know the four of you. You're good girls. Makes me think she also did more than a few things right. Try to remember more of the good stuff. Do you think you could do that, Sky?"

I wanted to, but I didn't honestly think I could.

Chapter 14

"Come on Brooky, time for bed," I said, putting down my book.

"Don't want bed," Brooky responded. She never wanted to go. Usually I had to lie with her until she fell asleep.

"Come on. I'll read you a story and —"

"Don't want you to read. Want Uncle Cole to read," she replied.

"Brooky, it's too late to argue and . . ."

"It's okay," Cole said.

I turned around, surprised to hear his voice. He'd been staring at the TV, not paying any attention to us. Brooke ran across the room to him and he scooped her up in his arms. She looked so little against him.

"Are you sure about this?" I asked.

"Sure I want to do it, or sure I know how?"

"Both." I couldn't help but smile.

"Sure I want to, and figure I know how to."

He'd been surprising me more and more. It wasn't just the things he was doing and how he was treating us, but the way he was thinking. At first he didn't seem too bright. Then, little by little, I realized that maybe he hadn't gone to school very long, and his grammar was terrible, but he wasn't dumb. He had a lot of things figured out pretty good, including me, and that bothered me. It was easier to deal with stupid people because they didn't surprise or trick you.

"Can I come and hear the story too?" Meadow asked.

"If you listen you have to go to bed too," Cole answered.

"No problem," Meadow said.

She stood on the couch and Cole picked her up in his free arm. Both girls started giggling. He had to turn sideways to carry them down the hall. He pushed open their bedroom door with the toe of one boot.

I turned to Summer. "You should have a bath and then finish your novel. When is your book report due?"

"Not for another week and a half."

"Good. Think how impressed your teacher will be when you hand it in early."

"Sky!" she protested.

"Summer!" I replied, mimicking her tone of voice. "Scoot! Now!"

She tried to fix me with an angry glare but it quickly dissolved into her familiar smile. She giggled and ran off to the bathroom.

I picked up my book, opening it to the spot where I'd stopped reading. I had a report due as well. Unfortunately mine was going to be turned in late. I shuddered, thinking about the hassle my English teacher was going to give me about it.

In the background came the sound of water filling the tub, punctuated by bursts of laughter from the bedroom. Obviously, the girls were enjoying the story. I wondered if he was reading them a copy of *Popular Mechanics* or a motorcycle repair manual. There was another burst of laughter. I put down my book. I had to see what was going on.

I tiptoed down the hall. The creaks of the floorboards were drowned out by the sounds of Summer singing in the tub. The bedroom door was slightly open. Cole was reading Brooke's favorite book, *Cinderella*. He was doing the fairy godmother part in a high-pitched voice, and I had to put my hand over my mouth to stifle a laugh. Both the girls started giggling again.

"Could we have one more story?" Meadow asked when he finished.

"Nope. Lights out." His feet clicked against the floor and the room became dark.

"No fair. Sky always sings us a song and lies down with us," Meadow protested.

"I'll get Sky," he said.

"No! No! You!" Brooky objected.

"But sing?" Cole asked.

"Yes, sing. Sing us a song," Meadow pleaded.

There was silence and then I heard the bed springs sag under Cole's weight. At first I could just barely hear his voice, then the words became louder and clearer. He was singing "Old Texas Town." I was stunned. That was the song my mother always sang to us.

I retreated back to the living room, my mind reeling. Why did he choose that song? How did he even know it? More important, why was he doing all of this? Being here with us was one thing. We hadn't talked about the deal since that first night in his apartment. It was one of those unspoken sorts of things. I'd put the terms on the table and he was holding up his end of the bargain. There was no need to talk about it anymore. But the deal didn't include making dinners, playing with the kids, helping to clean up or reading bedtime stories. It wasn't like Joanne was here to see any of this. Maybe he thought he'd get more money if he did more . . . or maybe he was starting to really . . .

"They're both asleep," Cole said, startling me out of my thoughts.

"That's good. Thank you."

"No problem," he answered.

"That song you were singing —"

"You heard me? I wasn't that loud," he said.

"Just a little, when I was passing by the door," I lied. "Why did you choose that song?"

"I don't know. It just kinda popped into my head. Haven't even heard it since I was little. I think my mamma used to sing it to me."

"Your real mother?"

"Yep."

"Maybe that's where my mom got it from," I said quietly.

"Ruby used to sing that song?"

"All the time when she was putting us to bed."

He smiled. "How long were you really listening at the door?"

"A long time."

"I figured. And how did I do?"

"Good. You did really good."

"I've had a good teacher," he said.

I was confused. "Who was your teacher?"

"You," he answered.

"Me?"

"Yep. You're really good with the girls. Just about the best parent I ever saw, at least up close."

"Thanks," I stammered. I felt myself blushing.

"With all the practice you've had with them, someday you're going to be just about perfect with your own."

"My own! I'm not ever having kids," I protested.

"Never?"

"Never! No way!" I almost spat the words.

Cole walked over to the fridge and opened the door. He grabbed a Coke, took a long sip and wiped his mouth with the back of his hand. I had to hand it to him. He hadn't brought a single beer into the house since we moved in. I guess he was doing his drinking elsewhere, probably when he went out every day to meet people.

"You shouldn't ever say never," Cole said.

"This is a never. No kids."

Cole started laughing.

"What's so funny?" I demanded.

"Always said I'd never have kids, but look at me now."

Chapter 15

"Mrs. Jenkins?" the PA crackled.

"Yes?"

"Sorry to interrupt, but is Sky in class today?" a woman's voice asked.

Mrs. Jenkins looked over at me. "Yes, she is."

"Please have her report to the office."

"Now or after class?"

"Right now. She's to see the vice-principal."

There was a rumble of response from the class. I swallowed hard. I'd been in a lot of schools and in none of them was a trip to the v.p. anything but trouble. I gathered my books and started for the door.

"Good luck — you'll need it," Vanessa said with a smile on her face. She didn't like me and I didn't like her.

"Meet you by the lockers?" Julia asked. Besides eating lunch together, we usually walked part way home. It was nice to leave the school with somebody and not have to walk alone through the hoards of kids loitering at the doors.

"I hope," I answered.

I closed the classroom door behind me. The hall was empty. The office was at the far side of the school, which would give me time to think. I'd already been given a warning for cutting classes before I started forging notes to excuse myself. I hadn't really done anything else wrong, except for maybe giving my English teacher a hard time. I had an assignment past due. It would be just like that old bag to report me.

The office was as crowded as the halls were empty. A thick wedge of kids was waiting at the counter and every available seat was already taken. It looked like I was in for a long wait.

"Sky."

I looked over at the secretary. "Yeah?"

"Come this way," she said, motioning me inside.

This was not a good sign. Hesitantly I made my way through the crowd as kids shuffled aside to let me by. This was the only place in the world, except for maybe death row, where nobody objected when you went in ahead of people who'd been waiting longer.

She knocked on the vice-principal's door.

"Come in," came the muffled response.

The secretary opened it. "Sky is here."

"Good, send her in."

The secretary smiled at me and walked away.

For a fleeting second I thought about escaping, but while I could run, I couldn't hide. Besides, what was the worst thing that could happen? I squared my shoulders and walked into his office.

"What are you doing here?" I asked in shock.

"Meeting with your vice-principal. Close your mouth and sit down," Cole said.

I plopped down into the chair beside him, speechless. This was unbelievable.

"Your uncle and I were having a very nice talk. Would you like to know what we were discussing?"

"Um . . . yeah, I guess."

"Yes, sir," Cole said.

"What?" I stared at him.

"Yes, sir, is what you call your vice-principal. Understand?"

"Um . . . yes . . . sir," I mumbled. This was getting too weird for words.

"I informed your uncle you were having some difficulties initially missing classes but that your attendance has greatly improved of late."

"I was glad to hear that," Cole said.

"And we also talked about the problems you're having with your English teacher. It seems there is a — how should we say it? — personality clash between the two of you. You don't get along very well, do you?"

"You can say that again," I answered.

Cole nudged me with his elbow and shot me a dirty look.

"Sir," I added.

"I also informed your uncle you failed to hand in a major assignment due last week."

I looked down at the floor.

"Your uncle explained to me the situations you've been through over the past few months. It must be hard, at times, for you to focus on school. In light of those circumstances I was prepared to arrange for you to transfer to another English class and to forget the missed assignment."

I kept my eyes focused on the floor, but my heart soared to the ceiling. I tried hard to keep a smile off my face.

"But he has convinced me that neither of those things are necessary or in your best interests."

"What?" I asked.

"Your uncle wants, and I fully agree with him, for you to stay in the same class and learn to deal with the teacher. I can assure you she is an excellent teacher despite the problems you are experiencing."

"You're joking, aren't you?" I asked.

"No joke," Cole replied. "You can't run from your problems. You have to learn to deal with them. There'll always be people you don't get along with. That ain't — I mean that isn't — no excuse to quit."

"And as for the assignment," the vice-principal continued, "your uncle has assured me it will be on Mrs. Riley's desk first thing Monday morning."

"And you be sure to thank Sky's teacher for giving her a little more time," Cole added.

"Certainly. I'll pass on your appreciation."

Cole rose to his feet and reached out his hand. The v.p. did the same and they shook hands.

"Is it okay if I take my niece home now rather than have her go back to class?" Cole asked.

The v.p. looked at his watch. "It's only ten minutes until dismissal. I don't see why not . . . especially since it's with her guardian's permission." He smiled.

"Come on, Sky."

"And Mr. Gray, thank you for coming down today. I just wish more parents were as reasonable and caring as you are."

"No problem."

Cole held the door open for me. Wordlessly I rose and left the office. This was like some sort of bizarre nightmare. What had just happened here?

"You feeling sick again?" Cole asked.

"What do you mean?"

"Like you were three weeks ago. You remember when you missed the afternoon of school and I wrote a letter to explain you were going to see a specialist?"

I swallowed hard.

"And I guess I must've been sick, too. So sick I

couldn't even remember writing the letter. Imagine that, huh?"

This was going from bad to worse. "Did you tell him?" I asked.

"The vice-principal?"

I nodded.

"If I had, would you have got outta there without a suspension? By the way, what did you do when you cut classes?"

"I . . . um . . . went to the movies . . . with some friends."

He nodded but didn't say anything.

There were a few more kids around now, going to their lockers, talking and getting ready to head home for the day. I couldn't wait to get out of here. Every head turned to watch us walk down the hall. I couldn't even imagine what they were thinking.

Cole pushed open the door and I followed him out. I was glad to get free of the building and the eyes watching us. His bike was parked up on the sidewalk. He stopped and I practically bumped into him.

"Do you know why this here wallet is attached to my pants with a chain?" he asked.

I was about to answer that maybe it was so that if it fell out of his pocket when he was riding he wouldn't lose it, but I didn't. Could he know? My heart skipped a beat before it started hammering away.

"It's chained down so it won't float away. You see it doesn't weigh that much. Matter of fact sometimes it doesn't weigh enough. A couple of weeks ago it got lighter by twenty bucks. And that ain't never going to happen again, you understand?"

He knew everything. I wanted to just crawl away and hide under a rock.

"Never again!" he repeated.

* * * *

The roar of the engine made conversation impossible. But for once, I appreciated the noise. The bike had hardly come to a full stop when I jumped off the back and stormed up to the house. I ran straight into my room, slammed the door, and buried my head under my pillow.

There was a knock on the door. I ignored it. I heard the door open.

"Get up."

I rolled over. "Get out of my room, now!" I demanded. "You have no right to be here, just like you had no right to come into my school today! What did you think you were doing?"

"According to your vice-principal, acting like a caring and responsible parent."

"Hah, maybe you had him fooled, and maybe you can even trick Joanne and the judge, but you can't fool me!" I snapped. "I know you're just in it for the money!"

"For the money," he echoed quietly, shaking his head.

"And don't think you can get more bucks for pretending better."

"You still think this is about the money."

"I don't think, I know. Why else would you be doing any of this?"

His face took on a frightening look. "There ain't nothing I'm going to say that'll make you think any different, is there?"

"Nothing at all."

He nodded his head slowly. "*Fine.*"

My mother's word and tone of voice. How dare he sound like her!

"Believe what you want, I can't change what's in your head. But get up, now, and start working on your assignment."

"You must be joking."

"No joke. You're going to do it."

"Why should I?" I demanded to know.

"Three reasons: it's past due, I gave my word you'd do it and because I'm telling you to do it."

"You're not my parent and I don't have to listen to anything you say!"

"That's where you're wrong. You do have to listen."

"And if I don't? What are you going to do?"

There was a pause. I had him there. What was he going to do about it?

"I'll leave."

"Big deal. You leave every day," I replied.

"I won't be coming back. I'll call Joanne and tell her the whole thing is over."

"You do that and you'll lose any chance at the money," I said defiantly.

"And you'll lose any chance at keeping your family together. I'm going to pick up the girls from school. You have till I come back to get down to work."

He turned and left the room. I sat in stunned silence and heard the front door slam shut. Who was he trying to bluff? The money was too important to him. He wouldn't risk losing it. He wouldn't . . . would he? I just didn't know — and I couldn't afford to take a chance. I grabbed my knapsack and pulled out the assignment.

Chapter 16

"Can I have the last one?" Meadow asked.

"No, me! Me!" Summer exclaimed.

"All of you be quiet. Bad enough you're stuffing your faces like pigs, you don't have to sound like a bunch of baboons," Cole said loudly. "So neither of you can have the last one."

"Who gets it then?" Meadow asked.

"Me!" Cole growled as he took it from the platter.

"That's not fair!" a few voices protested in unison.

"What's not fair about it? I did the shopping, I did the cooking and I'm the biggest, so I should get the most to eat!"

There was a storm of protest.

"Besides!" Cole yelled, silencing everybody. "It ain't the last one."

"What's all the fuss about?" Ed asked as he came in from the kitchen. He held another platter stacked with burritos. Everyone cheered and applauded. Then Cole gave one of his donkey laughs and everybody roared with laughter. Except me.

I hadn't eaten much. For the past two days I'd been too annoyed to want anything to do with him, including his cooking. It wasn't just his coming to my school that had me riled up. It was the way he was acting. He was telling the kids what to do more and more, like he really was in charge. And even worse, they were listening to him.

The scent from the plate of burritos swirled into my nostrils. It all smelled good, but I wasn't going to sell out for a few crumbs. Later on, after everybody had gone to bed for the night, I'd sneak into the kitchen and help myself to something to eat. Who knows, there might even be a leftover burrito or two.

Cole had gone out for a couple of hours in the afternoon. He said he had things to do, like usual on Sunday afternoons. Maybe he just needed to get away, take a break from being around us all the time. I could at least understand that.

I pictured Cole riding his bike down the highway, the wind in his face, free as a bird, speeding past cars like they were standing still. I wondered if he ever thought about not turning around, just riding away. I thought about him not coming back every time he left. It wasn't until I heard the bike roaring up the driveway that I relaxed. I don't know if the sound of his bike would ever be music to me, but it did bring a sense of relief.

I would have almost understood if he didn't come back. I knew how tired I was becoming of always having to be in charge, of watching everything, including him, and fearing that the whole thing could come tumbling down if we made even one slipup.

Ed got up from the table and started clearing away the dishes. I knew better than to help him. He insisted on earning his keep whenever he came for dinner. This meant he'd clear up and do the dishes while we watched television. Cole would go into the kitchen with him and sit and talk while Ed worked. I was amazed at how well the two of them got along. They were always gabbing away.

Despite the friendliness, occasionally I caught glimpses of them sizing each other up. Cole still was cautious around the ex-cop, and Ed never mentioned any of his concerns anymore, but I knew they were still in his head.

I had just chased Summer away to do her homework and got Meadow and Brooke settled into watching a kids video when the phone rang. Meadow reached over and grabbed it.

"Yep. He's here. Hold on." She laid the phone down on the coffee table. "Uncle Cole!" she screamed at the top of her lungs. "Telephone!"

Cole came through the swinging door. "Who is it?"

"Don't know," Meadow answered, her eyes focusing on the video.

"Probably somebody trying to sell me something," he said as he picked up the phone. "Yeah, what do you want?" he asked in a gruff tone. "Oh, hi. What's happening? Hang on a second." He picked up the phone and walked away, the long line stretching after him. He turned his back to where we sat.

"Okay . . . yeah . . . do you have any idea what you're doing?"

His voice had risen and he turned to see if I was watching him. I pretended I was ignoring him.

"Sit tight . . . yeah, yeah, I know where you are."

He hung up the phone and took his jacket off the back of the chair by the door. "Gotta go."

"Go where?" I asked before I had a chance to think not to ask him.

"Out."

"Out where?" Again the question popped out without my even thinking about it.

"Last time I checked I was the parent and you was the kid. Put the little ones to bed. I'll be back as soon as I can." He opened the door and was gone. Within seconds the Harley roared away.

Ed popped around the door. "Was that a Harley I just heard?"

I nodded. "Cole's Harley."

"Where's he going to?"

"Out."

"Where?"

"Don't know. Do I look like his parent?"

"Funny girl. You mean he didn't tell you?"

"Nope. He got a call. I don't know where he is or when he'll be back."

"Interesting," he commented as he went back into the kitchen.

I followed him. "What do you mean by that?"

"Oh, nothing. Just interesting, that's all."

"Interesting enough to mention to Joanne?" I asked.

"I don't know why I have to tell you things a second, or third, time. I'm not here to report things to Joanne." He paused, plopped the dishrag into the sink and looked me square in the eyes. "But you don't believe me, do you?"

I didn't answer.

"Then again, you don't trust anybody."

"I trust somebody."

"I meant other than yourself," he chuckled. "I'm on your side, Sky."

"Yeah, right."

"Sky, if I was going to tell Joanne anything I would have told her Cole is on the run from something."

"What makes you think that?"

"He had an unlisted phone number, signals to answer the phone, no name on the apartment nameplate, missing insignia on the jacket and the blocked-out tattoo you mentioned to me."

"So what! You were the one who ran the police check and he's not wanted by anybody!" I argued.

"All that means is he isn't wanted by the police."

"Then who'd be after him?" I questioned.

"Don't know . . . at least not yet."

I didn't like the way he answered the last part of that question.

* * * *

Ed took his time cleaning up. I think he was trying to hang around until Cole returned, and he didn't look comfortable leaving us alone when I finally pushed him out the door. I wanted Ed to leave in case Cole didn't come back till late. I was beginning to believe he wouldn't tell Joanne anything, but it was better if he didn't know anything anyway.

I tucked Brooke in bed by eight. Next came Meadow. She'd been wearing her uniform for the last four days and I needed to get those clothes into the washer. I wrestled her into her pjs and into bed. Summer was last. I helped her with her homework, had her read for thirty minutes and lay down beside her. Mom always used to lie down with her until she fell asleep and Summer insisted I do it now. I felt awfully tired and felt myself starting to drift off. I tried to fight it. I had too much work to do to . . . but the inviting warmth filled my body.

* * * *

I awoke, surprised to find myself beside Summer. I got up and checked the time. It was after midnight! I'd been asleep for more than two hours. I peeked into the other bedroom. Brooke was sleeping on her back, all rolled up in her covers like a little mummy. Winslow was tucked under one arm. Across from her Meadow was snoring away. The door to Cole's room was open and I looked in cautiously. He wasn't there.

I walked around the house turning off lights and then settled down in front of the television. I wondered if there was a good movie on. The phone rang and I was so startled I almost jumped right out of my seat. At least he was calling.

"Yeah," I snapped.

"Oh, I didn't expect to get you at this time of the night," Joanne said.

My heart skipped a beat and it took me a few seconds before I could talk. "Why are you calling so late?"

"It's just part of the supervision order. This is no different than the other calls and visits I've made. This one's just a little later. A better question is why are you up so late on a school night?"

"I, um, just got up to get a glass of water," I stuttered.

"Sure," Joanne answered, sounding totally unconvinced. "Let me talk to your uncle."

I took a deep breath. What was I supposed to do now?

"Sky, are you still there?"

I could hang up on her and then leave the phone off the hook so she couldn't call back.

"Sky?"

I could just tell her I was babysitting. Nothing was wrong with a fourteen-year-old watching her sisters. But what if she asked where he was, or what if he didn't come home at all tonight and she came over to check and . . .

"Sky?"

"Yeah, I'm here."

"Can you get your uncle please."

"He can't come to the phone right now. He's in the shower."

"At twelve-thirty at night?"

"Some people go to bed late. Besides, is being clean against the law?"

"Of course not. I guess I'll just talk to you until he's out of the shower."

"Not me. I've got to get some sleep. I have school tomorrow you know."

"How long is he going to be?"

"I don't know. He was fixing some bikes, and it's difficult to get all the dirt and grease off. Just call him tomorrow," I suggested.

"Sky, is your uncle out?"

"I told you, he's in the shower. Are you calling me a liar? Is that the way a social worker is supposed to talk to a kid?"

"Of course not, and I'm not calling you . . ." She paused. "Sky, I'm going to call back in twenty minutes. Either your uncle talks to me or I'm coming over there . . . tonight."

"Then call back in twenty minutes!" I slammed the phone down.

We were in big trouble now. I couldn't just sit here. I had to do something, but what? Where could he possibly be? The name Murphy's Bar came floating up from my memory. That was the name he mentioned the last time he ran out in the middle of the night.

I grabbed the phone book and sliced through the pages until I found *N*. I backtracked a few pages until an advertisement practically jumped off the page at me: *MURPHY'S BAR, cheapest draft in town, hot, hot chicken wings, big-screen television and absolutely no dress code.* This was just the sort of place Cole would hang out.

I dialed the number. "Come on, pick it up," I said as it rang and rang. Time was ticking away with each unanswered ring.

"Yeah?" a man's voice came over the phone. His response startled me.

"Um — is this Murphy's Bar?"

"Yeah, that's right."

In the background I could hear the rumbling of conversation and very loud music.

"I'm looking for somebody."

"Who isn't?" he answered. His voice was straining to speak over the noise.

"You don't understand. I'm looking for a man."

"Depending on what you look like, you may have found him, honey."

"I'm looking for my uncle," I stammered. "His name is Cole. Do you know him?"

"Lady, nobody knows nobody here. That's why people come here." Behind his voice came the sound of smashing glass and somebody cut loose with a stream of swear words.

"But it's important I talk to him. Very important."

"Told ya, I don't know the dude. 'Sides, how do you even know he's here?"

"I'll tell you what he looks like, then you can at least tell me if he's there, okay?"

"Shoot."

"He's really big, tall and thin and he has an earring, and a red bandanna and a leather jacket —"

"And ripped jeans and boots and tattoos on his arms," he interrupted.

"Yeah, that's him!" I exclaimed. "He's there!"

"Could be."

"But you just finished describing him."

"And half the people here. What do you think people in a biker's bar look like, suits and ties?"

"No, I just —"

"I gotta go, lady. I can't help you and I got beer to serve. This ain't a crowd you wanna keep waiting."

"But I need to know if he's there. It's important."

"You said that. What's so important, anyway?"

"It's his kids."

"What about his kids? Somebody been hurt?" For the first time he sounded concerned.

"Not hurt," I answered. "Worse than hurt. If he doesn't get home soon they're gonna be taken away by a social worker. His name's Cole."

"Hang on," he said.

I heard the background music suddenly die and a chorus of angry voices rose up in protest. "Shut up!" he yelled. "Have we got a guy named Cole in here tonight?"

I held my breath and waited. There was no sound at the other end. Then I heard the phone being picked up.

"Yeah . . . this is Cole."

I felt a rush of relief so profound I didn't immediately think to speak.

"Hello? Who is this?"

"It's me, Sky," I blurted out. In one long sentence, without stopping for breath, I explained everything to him.

"Not good," he answered.

"You still have about ten minutes. Come right now, quickly!"

"Can't get there fast enough. This place is over thirty minutes away. Can you stall her or something. "Tell her I'm in the shower."

"That's how I got this twenty minutes."

"Maybe I can beat her there."

"No chance. She lives only ten minutes away. Once she can't talk to you she'll be right over. She's probably getting ready right now."

"Well, I gotta try. I'll leave right now and —"

"No! I've got an idea, but it depends on two things. Can you use the phone there?"

"I'm using it now, what do you think I'm doing, yelling real loud?"

"Yeah, right. The second thing is can you get it completely quiet there?"

There was a long pause, too long for the time we had left. "If I have to."

"You have to."

"Then I can. What's your plan?"

"Hang up. I'm going to call you back from your business phone."

"Why? What's wrong with this phone?"

"Nothing, except that Joanne is going to call me back on this one."

"Don't see how that'll help."

"I'm going to put the two phones together, and if you talk really loud, she'll think you're right here. Joanne isn't too hard to fool. Unless you have a better idea."

There was another pause. "Call me back," he said. The phone clicked.

I ran into the kitchen and grabbed Cole's business phone. I came back into the living room and the line trailed out behind me. I dialed Murphy's

Bar and Cole answered. There was still lots of background noise.

"It needs to be quiet!" I hissed.

"Wait," he answered and he put the phone down. There was an incredibly loud crash, like the sound of smashing glass. I pictured a mirror being broken or glasses of beer being swept off a table. The crash was followed by angry voices and then, just as the other phone rang, it was quiet. I grabbed it.

"I thought you were going to give him twenty minutes?"

"I did, Sky."

"What do you have, a watch that tells time in dog years? There's no way it's been that long."

"Sky, let me talk to your uncle."

"He's just drying off, he'll be with you in a minute or five."

"Sky, either I talk to him right now or I'm coming over."

"Keep your shirt on, here he is," I said.

I muffled the receiver and picked up the business phone.

"Cole?"

"Yeah, who were you expecting?" There was no other sound except his voice.

"She's on the other line. I'm going to put the two receivers together. Talk loud, really loud."

"How else do I ever talk?"

I turned one receiver upside down and gently pressed the two together. I didn't want her to hear the sound of plastic hitting plastic. I pressed my ear close to the cuddling phones.

"What you getting me out of the shower for and keeping my niece up so late?" Cole boomed.

I smiled. This was a good strategy with Joanne, make her feel guilty about things.

"I'm sorry, it's just I didn't think —"

"You didn't think, period!"

"It's just —"

"It's just nothing! Keeping the kid up late, interrupting my shower, what garbage is this?"

"I'm sorry, I couldn't hear everything you said," she said sounding even more apologetic.

"What do ya want me to do, yell? I got sleeping babies here. You want me to wake them up too?"

"No, of course not —"

"Good! I'm going to bed, so that's the end of this here talking!" He slammed the phone down.

I listened, not even breathing, waiting for Joanne to hang up before she heard anything more from our end of the line. A few seconds later her line went dead as well. I took a deep breath and hung up both phones. Almost instantly one of them rang and I jumped into the air, recovering in time to grab it.

"Hey, Sky, pretty good acting job, eh? I don't think she'll ever be calling us late at night again. Got her so upset she don't know whether to spit or wind her watch."

"I think she fell for it."

"Missed my calling . . . should have been an actor instead of a biker."

He was some actor for sure. So good he almost had me believing him a couple of times. Before tonight he had me beginning to think he was starting to care for us . . . that we were more important than whatever he needed to do every night at some bar.

"We got her fooled for sure!"

"I think so," I answered icily. None of this would have been necessary if he hadn't been out boozing it up in some sleazy bar. Risking it all for a couple of drinks, or more likely, more than a couple of drinks, or worse yet, some drug deal or something.

"Sky, are you all right?" he asked.

I was surprised that he even realized I was upset.

"We fooled her. You go to bed, and I'll be there in a while."

"No rush. You've done your job. She won't be bugging us again tonight, so don't even bother coming home," I spat into the phone and hung up.

Chapter 17

Meadow and Summer were walking just behind me, and Brooke was sitting peacefully in the stroller. I hadn't slept more than a few minutes last night and I was always cranky when I was tired. To make it worse, I'd had a lousy day at school. A couple of the teachers had been nags, and then to top it all off, Vanessa and I got into a fight and we both got a detention, so I had to walk home by myself and was late picking up the kids after school. They all knew I wasn't in a good mood and they were giving me some space.

A group of kids were hanging out in the park. They were too far away to tell for sure who they were but that little kingdom was usually occupied by a collection of kids from my school. They spent most of their time being cool, usually by picking on others. Mom used to say you can't make yourself bigger by belittling other people, but it sure felt good sometimes to tear somebody down to size.

The kids started coming across the field toward us. I picked up speed, but I couldn't go any faster. We'd meet before we reached the street. I felt a growing sense of uneasiness. I hoped they were just heading home.

"Hey!" a voice called.

I had to fight the urge to turn around.

"Wait up!" called out a second voice.

"Sky, they're calling you," Summer said, pulling on my sleeve.

"Who cares," I snapped.

There were six of them. Four boys and two girls, including that little snot Vanessa and her friend Rachel. We had computer science and geography together. Not that either was there very often. They cut classes pretty regularly — even more than I did.

The two girls were dressed in identical leather jackets, black jeans so tight they looked like they were painted on and thick-soled, high-laced black boots. The foot gear alone was worth more money than my entire wardrobe. It sure cost a lot of money to look cheap and trashy. They stopped in front of us and formed a little semicircle.

The tallest of the four boys — Scott — stepped forward. He was a male replica of the girls except he had a cigarette dangling from his mouth. He was two grades and more than two years older than I was. Some of the girls at school were gaga over him. He had blonde greasy hair, and looked cool and confident.

"You live on Chambers Avenue don't you?"

"Yeah."

"That's my street," he said.

"All of it?" I asked in mock surprise. I wasn't in the mood to take any garbage from anybody.

"What did you say?" he asked.

"She was making fun of you, Scotty," Vanessa said. "I told you she had a mouth on her."

"Thinks she's better than us," added Rachel.

He seemed to ignore their comments as well as mine.

"And you go to my school."

"You own the school, too!" I mocked, clasping my hands to my face.

He looked even more confused. I was supposed to be all aflutter he was even talking to me.

He shook his head slowly and his smile turned to a smirk. "I wouldn't think anybody with a name like Sky would go around making fun of anybody."

The others giggled. Rachel looked at him with such adoration you'd think he just invented fire.

"Sky is a lovely name," Summer interjected. I felt myself cringe.

"Yeah, and what's your name?" asked Scott.

"I'm Summer and this is Meadow and Brooke."

"Meadow and Brooke? Sounds like one of those

nature magazines. What's the name of that one?" His expression changed. He looked like he was in pain or was constipated. It probably was painful for him because he didn't think very often. His expression suddenly brightened. "*Field and Stream!* That's it, *Field and Stream* . . . Meadow and Brooke . . . *Field and Stream!*" They all dissolved into a torrent of laughter.

I turned to Summer. "Take the kids home."

For an instant she hesitated like she was going to argue, but she sensed both my mood and the situation and started wheeling Brooke away.

"Where are they going?" Scott asked.

"Home. Where did you think they're going?" I replied. I knew the best way not to answer a question was to ask one.

The girls would be home in half a minute. I felt a shiver run up my back as I first sensed, and then saw, that they were shifting around until they completely surrounded me.

"So what makes you so special?" Scott asked.

I opened my mouth to answer when I was pushed from behind and almost fell into him. I tried to turn back around to face the source of the shove but I was hit again, this time from the side. I managed to regain my balance for a second before I fell to the pavement.

"I can take her," Vanessa spat out.

I knew she couldn't. She dressed tough but probably lived soft. Pretend punk. As I stood up to face her I was hit from behind and knocked right off my feet, my knees stinging as the asphalt bit into them. I had to fight to hold back the tears.

"How'd you like that one?" Rachel asked.

"If she can take me, why does she need you to help? Only babies need to have other people fight their battles for them!" I taunted.

Then I heard a familiar sound.

I looked up, and through Rachel's legs I saw the Harley bounce over the curb and come charging down the path. By the sound of the engine and the way he was closing in on us, I realized Cole was racing the bike at a tremendous speed. Everybody, including me, scrambled off the path. He roared past us, slammed on the brakes, spun the bike and came directly back at us, this time along the grass. He buzzed through the group and they scattered like an explosion. Once again he circled, and the bike tore a big piece of grass loose as the wheels grabbed for traction. He chased after one of the boys, cut around him, like a sheepdog chasing a sheep, and turned him back to where the others had gathered, huddled around a tree. Cole chased him until he joined the pack. He then stopped the cycle, turned off the engine, climbed off and jerked it back onto the kick stand.

Slowly and deliberately, he walked toward the group. I realized he wasn't wearing a helmet, just his bandanna. He motioned with his finger for me to come to him. I stood up. My knees hurt. One was scuffed up slightly but the other was bleeding badly. I limped over to his side.

"You okay?" Cole asked.

"I guess."

He nodded his head. "Go home."

"I'll ride with you, my leg hurts."

"I'm not going home yet. Go ahead, I'll be there in a minute or two."

"I'll wait."

I wanted to be there to see what happened next, but mostly I wanted to make sure he didn't do anything out of control. I'd seen what could happen when he lost his temper.

He shrugged. "Suit yourself."

He walked toward the group clustered under the tree. Scott came toward us, and the rest of the group followed behind. Scott's strut, which had vanished in the mad dash to escape the Harley, seemed to have reappeared. His boldness infected the others, and their posture changed as well.

"What's the idea, you could've hurt us!" Scott yelled angrily.

I couldn't believe it. This guy was so stupid he didn't even know enough to be scared.

"I *would* have hurt somebody if you all hadn't scattered like birds . . . actually like chickens."

"We weren't doing nothing, mister, why are you bugging us? We were just having some fun, that's all," Rachel said.

"Didn't look like everyone was having fun." He turned to me. "Were you having fun?"

It wasn't fun but I could have taken care of it myself. I didn't need anybody's help.

As everybody waited for my answer Cole bounded forward with a speed that astonished me. Everybody moved out of his way except Scott. Cole looked like he was going to strangle someone, but instead he just leaned almost right into Scott and stared him straight in the eyes.

"We're through talking. You're all goin' to listen. Understand?" he bellowed.

Scott, who was almost as big as Cole, stood motionless except for his nodding head.

"This here is my niece. Her name is Sky. Ain't that a pretty name?"

Scott's eyes seemed to widen but he didn't say a thing.

"I said," Cole repeated in a louder voice, "Ain't it a pretty name?"

Scott nodded emphatically.

"Good, glad you agree. Now I want you to know how much I 'preciate you being here to welcome my niece into the neighborhood. It's hard to be the new kid on the block. And I know you're goin' to help her settle in real good. You still following me?"

Scott nodded again.

"And you and your little buddies are going to be real nice to her. Fact is, you're gonna make sure everybody is nice to her." Cole stood up straight and moved back a step. Scott looked relieved.

"And you know why people are gonna treat her nice?" He didn't wait for an answer. "Because you're gonna make sure of it."

"Me?" Scott looked confused.

"You. You just been nominated to be Sky's bodyguard."

"I don't understand," he stammered.

"Then I'll explain it, 'cause I know you ain't stupid. You're a pretty tough guy, aren't you?"

"I guess," Scott replied.

"That's what I figured, and that's why you've been given the job. Matter of fact you're gonna make sure nobody bothers any of my nieces."

"But, how can I —?" Scott looked confused now.

"You can 'cause you got incentive. Anything happens to them . . . say like one of your little girl-friends bothers Sky . . . or somebody makes fun of her or knocks her books out of her hands . . . any-thing . . . and you and me'll be meeting again . . . and I won't be nearly this nice." He said the last few words so quietly that, besides Scott, I was pretty sure I was the only other person who even heard him. All of the others had been slowly, almost unconsciously, backing away to a safer distance.

Cole continued talking quietly. "And when I say meeting, you know what I mean, don't you?"

Scott nodded vigorously. Cole broke into a big smile and Scott smiled too.

"I know why I'm smiling, boy — so none of your friends think I just threatened you. You must be smiling because you think I'm joking. I'm not. Do I look like the kind of guy who has a sense of humor? Think about it." Cole paused. "Long enough. You gonna cooperate or —?"

"I'm going to cooperate. I promise!" Scott practically yelled.

"Good choice. Smart choice," Cole replied. He turned to where the others were huddled. He cocked a finger, motioning for them to come closer. They looked scared but complied, walking right up to him, staring at the ground.

"Your friend Scott, he's a pretty good guy. I want you all to know, and to let your friends know, that Scott and me is buddies. You mess with Scott and you mess with me. Same goes for Scott and Sky. Mess with Sky and you mess with Scott. Ain't that right, Scotty?"

"Yeah, that's right."

Cole reached out and shook Scott's hand. "Take it easy, man, and remember we got ourselves a deal."

I saw Scott wince, then he nodded and Cole released his grip. Slowly Scott curled and uncurled his fingers.

"Later," Cole announced and walked to his bike. Scott retreated toward the school, and the rest followed after him asking questions. I walked over to Cole who was climbing on his bike.

"What's with the deal part? Why are you going to protect him?"

"I'm not," he answered as he jerked the bike off the kickstand.

"Then why did you —"

"Only way he can protect you is if people think he's tough. Those kids saw him cave in to me. Word would've spread that he ain't much. So now kids'll think he's still tough and has an even badder friend. 'Sides, now the kid is still scared of me but figures maybe we's friends. Better to have him as sort of a friend of mine than an enemy of yours. Understand?"

"Sort of."

"It's all just psychology. You learn a lot of that on the streets or you don't make it." Maybe the words were different, but that was almost the same thing Ed had said to me about being a cop.

"Climb on," Cole gesturing to the back of the bike.

"No thanks."

"What do you mean, 'no thanks'? Your leg is hurt."

"It is, but I'd rather walk," I answered stiffly and walked away.

"Sky?" he called out but I didn't even turn around.

I heard the engine roar to life and the squeal of rubber on asphalt. The bike passed me in a blur as he raced along the path. He jumped the curb and onto the road, and turned out of sight. I limped home, alone.

* * * *

"That was a wonderful supper, Uncle Cole!" Summer exclaimed. "What do you call that?"

"Its name is hard to say. You just gotta know it's filled with hot peppers."

"Is it Mexican?"

"Farther south. A Spanish cousin from Chile."

"Chile food? That was the hottest thing I ever put in my mouth," Summer chuckled. "Get it, Sky?"

"Yeah, I get it," I answered coldly.

I stood up. I took my plate into the kitchen and dumped the food, almost untouched, into the garbage. My stomach was churning so badly I'd hardly eaten a bite. Returning for the next load of dishes, I saw Cole at the front door, putting on his coat. He was going out again.

"Get 'em all to bed. I won't be too late."

"Where are you going?" Finally I asked the question I'd wanted to ask all along.

"Out, like I told you."

"Fine," I snapped and went back to the kitchen.

I put the dishes in the sink. Cole came up behind me.

"Excuse me," I said, trying to move around him. He blocked me. "What's the idea?" I asked.

"What's your problem? Should I have just let

them beat the stuffing outta you?"

"I didn't need your help."

"Yeah, right! If I hadn't shown up you woulda needed the help of a doctor."

"I could have got out of it. I don't need your help or anybody else's!"

He stopped and narrowed his eyes. I could tell he was thinking.

"But you ain't mad about that are you? You're still steamed about last night?"

"That's right, and why shouldn't I be? I don't care what stinking business you're up to, but just don't do it when it's going to cost me my family!" I screamed. "Do your drinking or drug deals during the day when we're at school!"

"Is that what you think I'm doing? Going out to score or deal?"

"Yeah, that's what I think you're doing. I'm not the stupid one, you know!"

His face suddenly darkened and instantly I regretted my words — not that I didn't mean them, but out of fear of what was going to come next. I'd become so used to having him around, that part of me had forgotten just how big he was. Seeing him with those kids this afternoon, I remembered how dangerous he could be.

"Get your coat," he said.

"What?"

"You're coming with me." His voice was hardly a whisper and it sent a chill down my spine.

"I can't just leave the kids."

"Get your coat. I'll call Ed. He can come over and watch them."

"I'm not going anywhere."

"Either you walk beside me or I carry you out kicking and screaming. Don't make no difference to me."

"You wouldn't."

"Try me."

I knew he was telling the truth.

"I'll finish the dishes while we're waiting for Ed." I hoped that by delaying things I wouldn't have to go.

Cole grabbed my arm. "No time to wait. Can't be late. We're leaving now. Summer can watch the other two for twenty minutes."

* * * *

It took only two minutes for Cole to call Ed and for us to head out. I climbed onto the back of the bike and began a delicate balancing act, which wasn't easy with my sore knee. I didn't want to fall off the end, but I wanted to be as far away as possible from him. Cole's back blocked out most of the view, and what I could see was a blur.

I switched my mind from worrying about falling off the bike to worrying about what would happen if I didn't. Where were we going? What was I going to see? What was going to happen and what would the girls do if something happened to me?

I didn't have to wait long for the answer to my first question. He geared down and we bumped in to the nearly deserted parking lot of a shopping center. He drove slowly along the stores, their windows and doors locked and barred for the night. The lights in the parking lot provided only a dim glow and the headlight of the bike cut a path through the darkness. There were holes in the asphalt and Cole guided the bike around them. We rounded the corner of the mall. There were cars parked up tight to the wall where a light glowed brightly over a door. Cole brought the bike to a stop and we climbed off.

I was so scared I could feel my heart beating in my fingers. I looked up at Cole and was shocked to see he looked uneasy, too. Whatever was going to happen was even disturbing him.

"Come on," he commanded.

I followed him as he walked to the door. He opened it and then paused. "Keep your mouth shut."

I didn't need to be told a second time. I didn't think I could say anything anyway.

We went up a narrow set of stairs. The sounds of our steps echoed off the bare walls. At the top of the stairs was another door.

"Remember, shut up and you might learn something." He went through the door and it closed behind him.

I stood alone and tried to figure out what to do. Should I just stand there and wait? Maybe I should take off and get away while I had a chance.

The door opened below, followed immediately by the noise of feet against the stairs and loud voices coming toward me. I had my answer. I had to go in. I took a deep breath. I didn't know what was behind the door but I knew somebody was coming up behind me.

I pushed open the door and froze.

Chapter 18

"Please come in!" a woman called out from behind a podium at the front of the room. Between me and where she stood were rows and rows of chairs, most of them filled with people. There had to be close to fifty people, but where was Cole?

"Excuse me," came a voice from behind.

I jumped out of the way. It was a guy, maybe thirty years old, in a suit. With him was a woman who smiled at me as they passed by and took seats in the back row. Cole rose to his feet and motioned for me to come. I hurried over, brushing by other people in their seats to take the chair beside him.

The woman at the front began talking. I listened intently. She was going on about her life. It reminded me of those what-I-did-on-my-summer-vacation stories you have to write when you go back to school in September. I soon lost track of what she was saying and looked around the room.

There were dozens and dozens of people. They looked just like regular people, the sort you'd see in a supermarket. Men and women. Some were dressed in suits or fancy clothes while others were casual, and one couple looked down and out. Nobody except Cole was dressed like a biker. They ranged in age from only a few years older than me to really old. I didn't know what was going on here, but it sure wasn't a drug deal.

All at once the audience, including Cole, erupted in applause. The woman sat down and was replaced by a man at the podium.

"Thank you, thank you very much for your inspiring testimony," he said. "Now who would like to speak next?"

Cole rose to his feet. "Me. I want to go next."

I looked up at him in shock. Speak? What did he want to say? He shuffled sideways, and people in the row turned their legs to let him pass. He walked up the center aisle to the front, his heels clicking out that familiar rhythm. The man at the front patted him on the back and then sat down. Cole settled in behind the podium.

He cleared his throat. There wasn't another sound in the room. "Hello, everybody," he said quietly, "my name is Cole."

"Hello, Cole!" the entire audience responded.

"And I'm an alcoholic."

"Tell it like it is, Cole!" somebody yelled up from the audience.

Cole looked up and smiled nervously. "I've been here before. This is my ninety-third meeting in the last ninety-three days."

Most of the people clapped and others offered more words of encouragement.

"I've been sitting there and watching and going home and not drinking, but this is the first time I've said anything. It's time for me to talk."

He took a long pause and a shudder seemed to run up his whole body. He looked like he was about to cry. The man who'd been at the front rose from his seat and walked to Cole's side. He poured a glass of water and handed it to Cole. Cole took a sip and the man bent close and said something to him I couldn't hear. The man returned to his seat. Cole took a second sip and then put the glass down.

"I've been drinking and doing other stuff . . . drugs . . . since as long as I can remember. Maybe since I was thirteen or fourteen years old. There are days I don't remember. Heck, there are years that are just a blur to me. Just more booze to drown out my misery and take away my memories. And I've done some things I wish I could forget. Things I'm not proud of, things I wish I could take back or do over."

His voice was strained, and when he reached for his glass to take another sip, I could see his hand was shaking badly.

"I've been dry and clean now for ninety-three days. That's ninety-two days more than I can ever remember being dry. I know I just gotta take it one day at a time . . . that's what I keep reading about . . . that's what I keep hearing at these meetings . . . so all I can promise is I'll be dry today and try to be dry again tomorrow. And I make that promise to myself and I make that promise to my niece . . . who's with me here tonight."

I could sense eyes looking at me now. I tried only to look at Cole.

"I ain't got nothing more to say."

Cole walked away from the podium and the audience began to cheer. More than a few people rose to their feet, and Cole had to shake hands with people who crowded around him as he walked up the aisle. He finally found his way back and sat down beside me. He didn't say anything and I didn't know what to say to him.

Then that shudder I'd seen run through Cole's body worked it's way through mine and I couldn't stop myself from crying. Cole slipped an arm around me. I buried my face in his chest. His body began to shake as well, and I could feel the sobs erupting from inside him and heard him begin to cry.

Suddenly, another set of arms wrapped around Cole and me. I looked up. A woman, all dressed fancy, who had been sitting behind us, was holding on to both of us. Then another woman and a man both joined in. Somebody placed a hand on my head and people cooed words of support and encouragement.

"It's going to be okay ... everything is going to be okay," the woman said softly, and for the first time in as long as I could remember, I almost believed it.

* * * *

I stood at the back of the room and waited as Cole helped a few other men fold up the chairs and stack them over to the side. Glancing at my watch, I saw it was almost 10:30. The time had passed quickly as person after person talked about their drinking, and about the things that had happened in their lives and how they were trying to make a better life for themselves and their families without alcohol. The final chair was stacked and Cole walked over to me.

"Better be getting home," he said.

I nodded. "Why didn't you tell me?"

"That I'm an alcoholic? Hardly seems like something that would make people think any better about me."

"But why didn't you tell me where you were going, about these meetings?"

"Telling you I'm trying to live dry don't mean a thing. People been promising you things all your life and not delivering. I know you well enough to know you only believe what you see, and I wanted to have something to show you."

"Ninety-three days?"

"Yep. My last drink was the night you came to my old place. Been dry since."

"But . . ." I paused.

"But what about Murphy's Bar?" he asked, reading my mind. "I wasn't there to drink. I was there to stop somebody else from drinking. One of the guys I met here. We've become friends. He called me because he didn't think he could resist. Talked him out of it a couple of times."

"Was he here tonight?"

"Nope. Started drinking again, last night, before I got there. Nothing anybody else can do. Sometimes the alcohol is too strong and the will is too weak. That reminds me, how did you know to call me at Murphy's Bar?"

I blushed. "I overheard a telephone conversation once about you going there. I took a long shot."

Cole smiled and his blue eyes, my mother's eyes, gleamed. "That's what you figured I was, the longest shot. Come on, we better get home, it's getting late and Ed needs to get up early and play some golf tomorrow."

"Wait. I need to know, why — why you're doing this?"

"Had to stop drinking or I'd been dead."

"No, I don't mean about the alcohol, I mean about me and my sisters. Is it . . . for the money?"

"It never was about the money."

"Never?" I asked.

"I thought about it . . . I gotta tell you . . . I thought about it. Maybe in some ways it's because of the money I even stopped drinking."

"What do you mean?" I asked.

"When you came to see me that night and tried to bribe me to take care of you and your sisters, that was the bottom. How much lower could I be that you'd figure the only way I'd do the right thing was because of money. Can you imagine a man being so low?"

"I just thought —"

"You thought right and it got me thinking . . . about the four of you, bouncing from foster home to foster home . . . and I remembered what it was like . . . and I thought about how you were blood. My blood. I didn't figure I really had a chance to convince anybody to let me be a parent, but I knew I had to try and I knew I couldn't do it if I was drinking. I couldn't even take care of myself. And that's why. Okay?"

"Okay."

"Believe me?"

"I — I want to believe you."

"Good answer. Wait and see. I'll show you. Let's go home."

"Wait! I have one more question."

"Okay, shoot."

"What are you running from?"

A smile softened his face. "What makes you

think I'm running from anything?"

"Ed. He thought there was something."

He nodded his head. "Smart old bird. I didn't think he's stopped trying to figure things out. I am running . . . from my past. I was with a gang, a real bad bunch of guys, and I decided to leave."

"But why did you have to run? If you quit, you quit."

"It ain't that easy. Only way you leave a gang like the one I was in is if you go out feet first."

"What do you mean?"

"Dead. Lots of people I knew died. I should have been dead a dozen times before, myself. First time I realized I didn't want to be there anymore was when I thought the bikers who died were the lucky ones. They were free. So, one night I just got on my bike and rode. Left my place, all my things, even my clothes. Didn't tell anybody. Not even my old lady."

"You were married?"

"Nah, just a girlfriend. Left with just the clothes on my back. Rode for almost a full day before I stopped and stripped the patches off my jacket. I never looked back and I ain't never going back."

"But, but . . . is there a chance they'll be coming after you?"

"Nope. They probably think I'm dead the way I took off. And, I want to keep it that way. Nobody looks for ghosts. And it's funny, I really thought I'd come a long way when I left the gang. I was just so damn proud of myself for making some big changes in my life."

"And you did!"

"Only the start. I needed to hit rock bottom before I could start climbing back up. That night, while I was driving my bike back to my room after letting you off, I realized two things. How low I still really was . . . and the reasons I had not to give up. And I guess I owe you a thanks."

"What do you mean?"

"Just 'cause I've been dry for a while doesn't mean the alcohol still doesn't own me. A couple of times I figured I wouldn't be able to resist. You know, I got feeling sorry for myself, thinking about all the things that had gone wrong in my life. You'd know how that is, wouldn't you?"

Maybe better than anybody else in the world. I just didn't know anybody else felt the same way.

"But then I looked at you . . . never giving up . . . fighting to save your family and there was no way I could do any less." He paused. "And I guess I owe you something else." He reached into his pocket and took out his wallet. He removed a ten-dollar bill and handed it to me.

"What's this for?" I asked.

"Your allowance for this week. You deserve a few bucks each week . . . I'm sorry I can't give you any more."

"No, that's okay, I'm fine, really," I said, trying to push the money back into his hand.

"No, it isn't fine. I was wrong not to do this before. It was at least as much my fault as yours . . . you know, with the missing money."

I fell silent.

"Everybody, even you, needs a little break now and again. Come on now, let's go home . . . to our home."

* * * *

The lights glowed softly out of the living-room window, welcoming us as we pulled up to the house, our house. It felt good to be home.

"Where's Ed's car?" Cole asked.

It wasn't in the driveway. "Maybe he parked it on the street."

"Why would he do that?" Cole asked.

I didn't have an answer. "Look, there's a car over there," I pointed to the street. It was on the other side, in the shadows.

"Doesn't look like Ed's."

"Maybe he borrowed one or bought a different one," I suggested, although I didn't believe what I was saying.

I ran in to the house. Joanne was sitting in the easy chair. She rose to her feet.

"What are you doing here?"

Cole came in behind me and closed the door.

"I called earlier and found you'd left Summer in charge of Meadow and Brooke."

"We left Ed — I mean we called Ed to come and watch them."

"That's what Summer told me when I called but they were still alone when I got here. Ed arrived about an hour later. His car broke down and he was stranded. I sent him home."

Cole shrugged. "It won't happen again."

"You won't have a chance to let it happen again," she said, her voice cracking over the last few words.

"What do you mean?" An awful answer flooded my mind. I ran to the bedrooms. The beds were empty. Winslow wasn't even sitting on Brooky's bed. I staggered back to the living room, feeling like somebody had kicked me hard in the stomach. Cole was slumped in a chair.

"How could you do it?" I asked.

"It's my job . . . I'm doing what I have to do. You wouldn't understand, but I'm here to ensure the best care for you and your sisters."

"You can't make that decision!"

"I'm not. The judge ordered us to provide supervision. When I found the girls alone, I called my supervisor at home and she instructed me to take them into care." As Joanne talked she looked away from me. "Since we've apprehended the children, we have to go back before the court, tomorrow, to explain our actions."

"So we get to explain things to the judge. He can let us stay with Cole, can't he?"

Joanne nodded. "He can, but I don't think he

will. It's time for us to go, Sky."

"But — but I wasn't left alone," I objected.

"It doesn't matter. You'll be with your sisters tonight. I think they need you."

There was no point in arguing. She had the power to take me, and my sisters did need me.

"I had Summer pack you a few things, Sky. Your bag is already in my car. Court is at two o'clock. We'll see you there. Good night, Mr. Gray."

Cole didn't say a thing. He looked like a beaten dog.

Joanne walked to the door and opened it. "Come on, Sky."

"Just a minute . . . please. Could I just have a minute . . . alone."

She hesitated. "I guess that would be okay. And Sky, Mr. Gray . . . I really started to believe . . ." She paused.

I just glared at her. Empty words meant to somehow make it seem like she was less to blame for what she did.

She shook her head. "I'm sorry. I'll meet you by the car, Sky. Please don't be too long." She walked out and pulled the door closed behind her.

Cole sat silently on the chair. His legs were drawn up and his arms were wrapped around his knees.

"Cole, I'll see you in court tomorrow . . . right?"

"I don't know what good it'll do. We've lost."

"We have not!" I protested.

"Yeah right, we're winning real good."

"We can still win."

"Don't think so," he said solemnly. "They're not going to let us. My old man used to call me a loser . . . been losing my whole life, and I don't see it changing now. And you know what makes it worse is that I really thought we had a chance. At least if you know from the beginning you're going to lose you don't waste any time pretending or getting your hopes up. Nothing's changed."

"It has, I know it has." I paused as I tried to say what I was feeling in my heart. "We haven't lost . . . not yet."

I opened the door and stood there for a few seconds, trying to think of something, anything I could say. "I . . . I'll see you tomorrow."

Cole looked up but didn't answer.

Chapter 19

"What time is it?" I asked.

"Two fifteen, which is exactly two minutes later than the last time you asked me, girl," Mr. Bailey answered. "Besides, isn't that a watch you have right there on your wrist?"

Nervously, I pulled down the sleeves of my sweater — my mom's sweater. It was a little too small for me, but when I was getting dressed for court this morning, I knew it was the right thing to wear. Somehow I needed to bring a little bit of her with me. I didn't think her presence would help us to win but I wanted her there to comfort me if we lost.

"How much longer can you delay things?"

"Not much. Do you know if he's coming? No point in delaying if he isn't. Just gets the judge annoyed."

"He's coming. I'm sure he is. Ed's out there right now trying to find him."

I was so grateful for Ed. He was upset his car breakdown had led to court. I knew it wasn't his fault, and he knew it as well, but he still felt badly. If it was anybody's fault it was mine. Why hadn't I believed Cole? Why did I make him have to show me?

"If you're so sure he's coming, how come your friend has to be out lookin' for him?" Mr. Bailey asked.

Before I could answer, I spied a court attendant coming across the waiting room toward us. I hoped he was looking for somebody else or was going to the washroom. He stopped right in front of us.

"Mr. Bailey, we have a full docket this afternoon, so I'm afraid we have to commence."

"If you have a full docket then the judge can hear another case and we can wait."

"I'm afraid not. The judge has personally asked for this matter to be the first of the afternoon session."

"Well, I'm afraid he'll have to wait. I must consult with my clients and —"

"It's okay." I nudged Mr. Bailey. Cole's head and shoulders appeared above the crowd in the packed waiting room.

As he got closer I was shocked by his appearance. His hair hung down in tangled strands, he hadn't shaved and his eyes were red. Even his boots were coated with a thick layer of dust and dirt. I doubted he'd slept last night and I was afraid he'd been drinking. He looked like an unmade bed. Summer and Meadow saw him, too, and ran to him. I walked slowly and carefully, like I was approaching some skittish animal I didn't want to chase away.

"You're just in time," I said reassuringly.

"I'm late."

"Only a few minutes."

"Nope . . . years."

"No time for gabbing!" Mr. Bailey exclaimed. "You still wantin' the girls?"

"Do I have a chance?"

"I'm not a psychic, I'm a lawyer. Still want to try?"

There was a pause that seemed to last forever. Summer and Meadow looked up at him expectantly. He nodded and the tension dissolved into smiles. A small smile even crept onto Mr. Bailey's face.

* * * *

The only sound was the shuffling of papers as the judge read the affidavit the child-welfare lawyer had given him. Mr. Bailey had a copy as well and I caught little bits as he flipped through the pages. But it was written in lawyer language and I couldn't make much sense out of the little I was able to read. It was probably just fancy talk to say Cole shouldn't be our parent. A few times the judge stopped reading and looked at us, sitting beside Mr. Bailey. I tried to read his expression but I couldn't. Finally he cleared his throat, and everybody took that as a signal he was about to talk. I looked over at Joanne. She gave me a small, sad smile. I felt a twinge of remorse for her. She looked like she was the one being taken away from her family.

"Mr. Bailey, you have had an opportunity to read the affidavit prepared by the agency. As you are aware, they felt it necessary to apprehend the children due to lack of supervision. What is the position of your clients?"

Mr. Bailey rose from his seat. "I've had an opportunity to discuss this matter with the three oldest girls, and they remain certain they wish to be returned to their uncle."

"And Mr. Gray, are you still wanting to raise your nieces?"

"Yep. More than ever before."

The judge nodded solemnly. "There is no middle ground or room for compromise here. This matter will have to be adjourned for a full trial. How long will it take for you to prepare your case, Mr. Bailey?"

"Three or four weeks will be sufficient."

"And the agency? Is that enough time?" the judge asked.

The agency lawyer and Joanne put their heads together and talked quietly before the lawyer rose to her feet. "No, Your Honor. We require more time. We request an adjournment of at least six weeks to allow us to fully prepare our case."

"Six weeks!" I said out loud. Mr. Bailey put a hand on my arm to silence me.

"I must agree with the young woman's objection. That does seem like a long period of time," the judge replied.

"With all the demands made on the time of the social worker it's not possible to prepare for this matter any sooner. As well, the agency is still pursuing the children's fathers," the lawyer explained.

"I think that pursuit is without purpose," the judge said.

"But by law we are required —"

"Yes, I am *somewhat* aware of the laws," the judge said with a hint of sarcasm in his voice. "But, regardless whether you find the missing fathers or not, the girls will not support any plan that calls for them to be separated. Is that not correct, Mr. Bailey?"

"Completely correct, Your Honor."

"And in the interim? Where do you propose the children reside?" the judge asked the child-welfare lawyer.

"In foster care of course, Your Honor."

"What foster home? They'll probably throw us into three or four different places," I muttered.

Mr. Bailey nodded. "One of my clients wishes to know what foster home the agency presents as being their placement. Will the girls be in one setting or separated yet again?"

"And the answer to that is?" the judge asked.

"Um . . . perhaps the social worker can answer that best," the lawyer replied uneasily.

Joanne rose to her feet. "We are not able, at this time, to tell the Court where the girls will be. They were placed together last night in an emergency setting but will have to be moved."

"And separated!" I spat out.

Mr. Bailey shot me a dirty look.

"We want to be with our uncle!" I said loudly. "And no place else!"

Mr. Bailey rose to his feet. "If the agency wishes to delay the trial, an unreasonable delay I might add, and they cannot guarantee the children will reside together, I propose that during the period of adjournment they reside with their uncle."

"We strongly object!" the agency lawyer practically yelled.

"I'm afraid, Mr. Bailey, I must agree with the agency. Regardless of where the children will be placed, we must be assured they will be given adequate supervision and not be left alone again."

"That wasn't his fault!" I said.

The judge looked squarely at me. "You seem to have a lot to say. Did you have something you wanted to add?"

"No," I mumbled under my breath, looking down at the table.

"We're deciding your future, young lady, you should have a say in it."

"I said —"

"Stand up," Mr. Bailey whispered at me.

I rose and the chair scraped against the floor. "It wasn't his fault."

"Then whose fault was it?"

"Nobody's, really."

"Please explain," the judge requested.

"We called our friend Ed, and he was on his way over, but his car broke down. The kids were only going to be alone for about twenty minutes and Summer is ten and old enough to watch them for twenty minutes."

"Wouldn't it have been wiser to wait for this Ed to arrive?" he asked.

I paused. "We had to leave so we wouldn't be late."

"Late for what?"

I didn't know what to say. I stood silently.

"For my Alcoholics Anonymous meeting," Cole announced from the row behind me. I swiveled around to look at him. "Sky came with me to my meeting."

"Mr. Gray, since your position is one with those of the children, I would like you to come forward and take a seat at the front beside them and Mr. Bailey."

His boots clicked as he came forward, stopping when he was beside Mr. Bailey.

"How long have you been involved in AA?"

"Ninety-three . . . I mean ninety-four days."

"And your last drink?"

"Ninety-five days ago."

"Your Honor, this provides us with even more reason to oppose the temporary placement of the children in the care of Mr. Gray. Ninety or so days is insufficient time to provide evidence he has been cured of his drinking problem," the agency lawyer objected.

Cole laughed and shook his head.

"You have a response, Mr. Gray?" the judge asked.

"It's just that was a pretty stupid thing to say. Don't matter if it's ninety days or ninety years, you don't never cure it. I'm an alcoholic. Will be my whole life."

A slight smile creased the judge's face. "Do you have anybody from AA who can come and speak for you?"

"My sponsor. I guess I could get him to come."

"That would be appreciated. And what of this person whose car broke down? Is he here today?"

"Nope, he isn't," I answered.

"Yes, he is!"

I turned around. Ed was standing in the aisle right by the doors. He must have come in after court started.

"You look familiar to me. Have you been before my court before?" the judge asked.

"Never been in this court before, but we've met," Ed said. He walked down the aisle until he stood just on the other side of the swinging gate.

"And where would that have been?"

"Criminal court. I've testified in more than one case when you were a defense lawyer, before you got to be a judge. I helped send some of your clients to jail."

The judge smiled. "That's it . . . I'm sorry I don't recall your name but I do remember you now."

"That's okay. It's Ed, and that was a lot of years ago. Can I explain what happened, Your Honor?" Ed asked.

"Please."

"It's all my fault. My car broke down right in the middle of no place. Instead of being there in twenty minutes, it took me over an hour to even flag down a car and get help. I was ninety minutes late. I should have known better than to travel around in a beaten-up old car. I was being a fool."

"I remember my clients calling you a number of things, but never a fool," the judge replied.

"Like I was saying, none of this was Cole's — I mean Mr. Gray's — fault. As far as he knew I'd be there a few minutes after he left. And, if you don't mind my opinion on this one, I don't think it's against any law to leave a ten-year-old in charge of her two little sisters for twenty minutes, now is it?"

"I have to agree. And do you feel that you can also speak for Mr. Gray, as a character witness?"

"Well," Ed began. "There's no one in the courtroom who wouldn't agree he's a character all right."

Everybody, including the judge, chuckled.

"And, you'd have to have your head examined not to think that maybe this wasn't the best place in the whole world for these girls to be living and there's more things I don't know about Cole than I do know . . . "

What was he saying? Why was he doing this?

" . . . but it seems to be working. Cole's trying hard. He'd never do anything to hurt his girls. That I'd stake my life on."

I felt a rush of relief. For the first time since last night I felt a flicker of hope.

The agency lawyer stood up. "Well, I don't believe we're putting this to a vote. And, as we've outlined, we have grave concerns regarding Mr. Gray's numerous charges. Particularly those that involve fraud and other money-related crimes."

"All of this is history, Your Honor. All these objections were raised at the time of the previous court hearing, before the girls were placed in their uncle's care," Mr. Bailey responded.

"But also noted in the affidavit are our other concerns. Aside from the supervision issue, and it is even more serious than we realized now that we are aware Mr. Gray leaves the children unsupervised every day —"

"He does not! I'm always there when he goes to the meetings, and he's only gone for a little while!" I said indignantly.

"Whatever," the agency lawyer said. "Now we have even more serious concerns regarding Mr. Gray's alcohol abuse. And if he chose to hide this from us, and from the Court, we wonder what other skeletons are hiding in his closet. Perhaps there are criminal charges we are unaware of, perhaps his intentions are not so honorable, perhaps he is after the money from the lawsuit —"

"Your Honor, I strenuously object!" Mr. Bailey practically yelled.

"Please, Mr. Bailey, they are simply raising legitimate concerns."

"I don't want the money," Cole said solemnly, looking straight at the judge for the very first time.

"You don't?" the judge quested.

"Nope. Lock it away until the girls need it, when they're grown up." He paused and looked at me. "All of it."

"Very noble," the agency lawyer said. "But as they say, talk is cheap. Will Mr. Gray sign papers, here today, relinquishing all rights to the money and placing it in a trust until the children turn eighteen years of age?" It was clear that she didn't believe Cole would really give up title to the money and she was trying to call his bluff.

"I'll sign anything you want."

"What?" the lawyer looked shocked.

"How many times do I have to say it before you understand?" Cole asked.

The courtroom was dead silent as we all watched the judge. His eyes were focused on the back of the room and I could tell he was thinking . . . about the future of my sisters and me.

I looked at the agency lawyer who was flipping through her papers. A smile slowly came to her face and a shiver ran down my spine. She stood up.

"Your Honor, we have one more factor that needs to be addressed before you make your decision."

The judge peered at her.

"Mr. Gray has agreed to remove claim to any part of the money, with the full amount being put in trust. Is that correct?"

"I believe we've established that, have we not, Mr. Gray?" the judge asked.

"A few times."

"Well," she began again, "that is certainly very noble, but according to the information Mr. Gray previously put forward, he hardly has the income to support the children or to even put a roof over their heads. In all seriousness, Your Honor, you cannot suggest placing the children in an environment where basic food and shelter and clothing could be denied them and —"

"This is crazy, man!" Mr. Bailey thundered, jumping to his feet. "First you're sayin' he can't have the kids because he's a criminal and only wants their money, and then when he tells you he doesn't want any of the money, you say he's too poor to raise them! He's been raising them fine for over two months."

"Mr. Bailey!" the judge stated firmly. "Please control yourself . . . even if you disagree, totally, they are entitled to make their case."

Mr. Bailey's eyes flashed with anger and I could see his hands were drawn tightly into fists, but he remained silent.

"How will you provide for the girls, Mr. Gray?"

"The way I've been providing for them the last couple of months. I'll make sure there'll always be food on the table, a roof over their heads and clothes on their backs. May not be fancy clothes or the best place or expensive food, but I'll make sure they have what they need. You gotta remember, Your Honor, the thing they need the most is to be together . . . and I'll work my hardest to make sure this isn't only the best place they can be, but the only place they'll ever be."

"Very touching," the agency lawyer said sarcastically, "but what if for some reason Mr. Gray becomes unemployed or injured, or starts drinking again. He doesn't even have a cent to back him. He has absolutely no assets."

"I can sell my bike."

I looked at him in total shock. His bike! He talked about it the way other people talked about their kids. He loved it like he loved nothing else . . .